AMY ROBINSON

WITH ILLUSTRATIONS BY
DAVE HINGLEY

BASED ON A FOLK TALE RECORDED BY
WH BARRETT

THE FIRST KING
OF ~~ENGLAND~~ in a DRESS!

Enjoy joining in!

A(me)B xx

Snail
Tales

First published 2017

Snail Tales
43 Norfolk Road, Wyton
Huntingdon, Cambridgeshire PE28 2EF

British Library Cataloguing in Publication Data.
A catalogue record for this book is available from the British Library.

ISBN 978-1-9997523-0-9

Typesetting and origination by Snail Tales
Printed in Great Britain

For Matthew and Rachel.
Amy

For David and Patrick.
Chip

For my gorgeous fiancée, Vicki.
Dave

Love stories?

So do we!

Join our mailing list to get
free stories, free storytelling videos,
news about when we're storytelling near you,
special offers, *and* a free ebook
– and no spam ever!

Details at the end of
The First King of England... in a Dress!

CONTENTS

There's No Place Like England	6
The Viking	10
Ethelred	16
The Coalminer and the Frost Giant	20
Keku the Frog	29
A Hill Outside the Window	43
Secrets	46
A Not Very Nice Story	50
Another Not Very Nice Story	56
Making a Plan	60
To Ely	67
Monks and Vikings Aren't Best Friends	73
Naming the Land (well, kinda...)	81
One Big Problem	85
The Potion of Poetry	90
Disguises	103
Thor's Stolen Hammer	110
A Dress	120
A Song	127
Naming the Land (properly this time)	132
Into the Abbey	139
England	151

Bonus Features

Fact or Folklore?   160
About the Characters   163
About the Stories   168
About the Storytellers   171
How We Wrote This Book   176
Thank Yous   182

THERE'S NO PLACE LIKE ENGLAND

Many years ago, an English man was walking along beside a river in England.

No, wait. Most of that sentence isn't true. Let me try again.

First of all, it wasn't just many years ago. It was around 1017AD, which means the man couldn't have been beside a river in England – because

England didn't exist one thousand years ago.

I mean, the thing we call England – the big patch of land on the greenish island which is shaped a bit like a witch on a broomstick if you include the bit we call Scotland – *that* existed. But it wasn't England in those days. It started out as a jigsaw puzzle of lots of smaller countries, each with their own kings.

Some of those kings were Saxons, who came from Europe. Some were Angles, who also came from Europe. And some were Vikings, who came from Scandinavia – which is more or less the same thing as Europe.

Wherever they came from, though, these kings and small countries were always fighting each other, trying to make themselves a bit bigger and a bit more important.

A king called Alfred eventually got slightly further than the others, and managed to stick all the Angles and Saxons together. First they were known as the Anglo-Saxons. Later, they became known as the English.

Alfred's grandson, an English king called Ethelstan, fought the Viking kings and won, which meant he got to call himself "King Of All The English And The Vikings" – for about ten years. Then a Viking king got the north back – for about ten years. Then an English king got the north back – for about... Yes, well, you get the picture.

Part of the problem was probably that, in the time it took to declare "I am the King Of All The English And The Vikings!", your enemies found a way to sneak in and bop you on the head before you finished speaking.

At the beginning of our story, the King Of All The English And The Vikings happened to be a Viking – but the English and the Vikings still did not like each other one bit.

Anyway. Back to that first sentence. I told you "an English man was walking" – but if I'm honest, that's not true either. In fact, this man was actually a Viking. However, he was wearing a cunning disguise. He had dressed like an English man, because he was walking through English territory and didn't want an angry gang of English men to bop him on the head – or worse...

Do you know how to tell English clothes from Viking clothes? It wasn't a huge difference. Normal English and Vikings both wore plain shirts and trousers made of wool, with a tunic over the top – kind of an extra long shirt that went a little bit past the hips. They would hold all their clothes up with leather straps.

Even their shoes were similar: hard flat cuts of leather. They might also wear woollen hats (which looked a bit like extra-long beanies). It didn't really matter if you were male or female – nearly all men and women looked the same (except lords, ladies, queens, kings, nuns, and monks of course).

However, Vikings tended to care more about what they looked like. So, to make himself seem more English, all this Viking had needed to do was make his clothes dirtier, mess up his beard a bit, and occasionally mutter something like, "Bothersome Vikings, grrr..."

I was also wrong when I said this man was walking. The land he was travelling through was known as the Fens: a flat, flooded, marshy mud bath. Can you imagine walking through a swimming pool filled with baked beans? It was a bit like that.

So my first sentence *really* should have read, "About a thousand years ago, a Viking man disguised as an English man was squelching, sinking, slurping, splashing, and sloshing in a general forward direction, beside a river – which wasn't in England, because there was no place like England about one thousand years ago."

But that wouldn't have been very elegant, would it?

THE VIKING

It could be dangerous walking through the marshes. One wrong step and you could easily slip, and maybe drown. It was getting dark, and the Viking at the beginning of our story was finding it harder to see where he was going.

Just then, he spotted a small house – an English house. Maybe, just maybe, they would let him stay the night – as long as they didn't work out that he was really a Viking...

However, it was that or get stuck outside in the marshes all night – and drown, starve, or freeze to death.

So the Viking went up to the house, his feet squelching as he approached...

ETHELRED

It's a nearly normal evening. About as nearly normal as it has been since the worst day of my life. I'm sitting at the table cleaning my eel spear, like I do every night. Dad chops up the eels we've caught and makes them into a stew, like *he* does every night. You know, there's nothing like tucking into eel stew right after picking bits of dead eel out from between the mud-caked prongs of a giant fork. We Anglo-Saxons know how to live.

So everything is nearly normal.

Until the knock on the door.

I don't move – I think I've stopped breathing. Dad goes to answer the door, and he stands there a bit too long – letting the misty, marshy fenland air drift in and make me shiver.

"Who is it, Dad?" I ask, trying not to let my voice come out all high and trembly.

Dad glances at me over his shoulder. "He sounds like a Viking."

My first reaction is relief. I know that's silly, don't get me wrong. I know that Vikings are fierce, mean bullies who want to take our land away from us – like the new "King Of All The English And The Vikings", King Knut. I've never seen him, but I bet he looks like an ogre. And I know that if a Viking really did knock on our door in the dark – unlikely though that is – we would be in trouble. At least, we would if he was bigger than Dad, or if he'd brought any friends along.

It's just that *now*, I also know there are worse things than Vikings.

Still, the relief only lasts a few seconds. This mysterious man tells Dad he's definitely English, and he's been visiting his family near Ely. I'm not convinced one bit – but, to my surprise, Dad is. Dad actually decides to let this person in!

And, as if that weren't enough, Dad then goes into the next room to finish cooking – leaving me alone with Mystery Man.

I grit my teeth and tighten my grip around the spear. Mystery Man is filthy and sweaty, but there's something about his eyes... It's like he's more awake than any Fenman would normally be this close to night-time.

He says he's a lost English man called Edmund – and, clearly, he wants to have a conversation.

"So, boy," he says, in that fake cheerful voice grown-ups do when they want you to join in. "Ethelred, was it?"

Hopefully if I don't reply, he'll give up.

"What's that thing you're cleaning?"

I thought he told Dad he had been visiting his family round here. What kind of a Fenman doesn't know an eel spear when he sees one?

"Let me guess. Is it... a fork for eating food you've dropped on the floor?"

Ah, I get it now. He's teasing – trying to be cute to get me to reply.

"I know! It's a comb for hairy ogre toes!"

Gross.

"Wait! I've got it this time, I'm sure. It's a moon picker for gathering sky cheese!"

I fix him with my best unimpressed face. "It's an eel spear. For catching eels."

"Right. Of course." Edmund scratches behind his ear. "So, does your dad always do the cooking round here, or does your mum help? Where is she?"

I stare hard at the spear and pick off an invisible bit of eel skin.

Edmund sits down and sighs. My spear is cleaner than it's ever been, but I'm still polishing. I've never wished for eel stew to be ready so much in my life.

"The Fens are very flat, aren't they?" remarks Edmund. "Flat and wet."

"Well, duh."

He's unstoppable. "Want to know how they got to be so flat and so wet?"

"No."

"Oh. Well. Then I won't tell you about the coalminer who had to fight a frost giant."

I know a lot of stories, but I've never heard *that* one before. "The coalminer who had to fight a *what?*"

"A frost giant. A giant made completely out of ice," says Edmund. "You see, it was like this..."

The Coalminer
and the Frost Giant

Many years ago, the Fens weren't flat like they are now. Instead, there were hills as far as the eye could see – which wasn't very far, because of all the hills! Unless you were a bird, of course. Then you could see hills scrunching up the land for miles and miles and miles.

Each hill was made with a different kind of rock: coal, which was good for burning fires... flint, which was good for *starting* fires... and gems, that glittered and sparkled like fires...

At the start of this story, a miner was digging into the side of a hill for coal. He decided to dig deeper than any miner had ever gone before – and he didn't stop until his spade hit something extra hard.

He bent down with his burning wooden torch to get a closer look... then almost fell backwards in amazement. There at his feet was a gem – a gem sparkling brighter than any gem he'd ever seen before!

Excitedly, the coalminer began digging around the gem to get it out. As he did, he realised he had dug into an underground cave full of these dazzling gems. Since he was the first man to discover them, he needed to give them a name. What could he call them?

"Die, man!"

The coalminer smiled. "Yes, diamond! That's a great name! Thank y–"

Then the miner paused – and gulped. Whoever had spoken to him did not have a normal voice. It sounded too deep, too rough, and too *loud* to be a normal man.

Slowly, the miner turned around...

...and there, looking down at him, was a giant made completely out of ice: a *frost giant!*

With a long purple tongue, the frost giant licked its thick blue lips. Its icy skin shimmered and crackled as it lifted one arm and pointed at the coalminer – then...

ZAP!

...a bolt of lightning shot out from the giant's finger! It was too fast for the coalminer to jump out of the way, and the bolt hit his torch. Instantly the flame of light disappeared, and the coalminer was plunged into darkness.

Having seen the giant lick its lips, the coalminer was in no doubt about what the giant wanted – so he turned and ran as fast as he could. But he couldn't see where he was going, and the ground shook every time one of the giant's heavy feet landed behind him. He panicked: how could he run faster than a giant?!

Just then, his shoulder brushed against a wall in the cave – and he felt a gap. He quickly clambered inside, hoping the hole was too small for the giant to claw him out. Then he took two flints from his pocket to relight the fire on his torch. Each time he rubbed the flints together, a small spark shot out:

Scrape... scrape... WOOMPH!

A flame finally jumped up from the torch, and

the miner held it up to see where he was... and saw, right outside his little hole, a huge icy eye peering in at him!

But the giant staggered backwards – almost as if it was suddenly afraid...

Of course! The miner realised: the frost giant was scared of fire! It didn't want to melt!

As the giant moved back, the miner saw those gems sparkling magnificently again – revealing a way out! The miner took his chance, and dashed towards the tunnel to the surface.

It wasn't long, though, before the ground shook again – the giant was chasing him! Escape was surely impossible. So as the coalminer scrambled outside, he looked around frantically for a place to hide.

He spotted a forest nearby, and sprinted towards it. As soon as he felt twigs and leaves under his feet, he buried himself beneath them. Hopefully they would cover him enough to shield him from the sight of the frost giant...

The ground stopped shaking as the giant stood outside the tunnel, looking around for the coalminer.

"Where are you, man?"

The shaking began again – but the thumps seemed to get quieter, making the coalminer think the giant was moving away. Nervously, he looked out from his leafy cover.

Fortunately, the coalminer was right – the giant was moving away. But *un*fortunately, it was stomping the hills deep into the ground as it went, leaving nothing but flat land behind it.

The coalminer realised many human lives were in danger with the giant stomping around. But how could a little coalminer stop a frost giant?

Just then, he had an idea. Still holding his wooden torch, he climbed to the top of a tree and yelled: "Oy! Frosty! You're nothing but an overgrown *snowman!*"

The giant paused. It turned to face the coalminer, gave a bellowing roar... then charged towards the forest!

The coalminer only had a few seconds to act. He thrust the burning end of his torch into the branches beside him, then leapt down to the forest floor – landing hard but safely in a pile of leaves.

The fire in the branches spread from that tree to the others nearby... then more trees... then more...

The giant only noticed the fire as it got close to the forest – and by then it was too late. The giant tried to stop itself, but tripped and fell into the fiery trees. Flames wrapped around its icy body – and then...

Boooooom!

The frost giant exploded into a huge shower of water! The coalminer began running away as fast as he could – but, just a few moments later, he was swimming as fast as he could! Water rushed across the land flattened by the giant's feet, until it eventually crashed into the hills of the north, east, south and west.

When the waves finally calmed down, everyone called the coalminer a hero: his quick thinking had saved everyone from getting squished into the earth.

But all that water, the remains of the frost giant, sank down into the ground – creating the flat marshes we see all around the Fens today...

*   *   *

After Edmund's got his breath back, he gives me a grin. "So? Good story?"

I shrug. "It was alright. It's just–"

"Oh, come *on!*" he blurts. "Only 'alright'? What was the matter with it? When my aunt first told me that story, I–"

He suddenly stops, and frowns – almost like he's just thought that I don't care about him or his silly aunt.

And I don't. But I suppose I should be grateful

that he's trying to be friendly, and not burning our house down like the Vikings would. And he's taught me a new story. I do like stories.

So fine. I'll have a go at being friendly too.

"Yeah? Who's your aunt? Is she the one you've been visiting?"

"Never mind. I interrupted you. What were you going to say?"

"Huh? Oh. Nothing really. Just that it obviously isn't a *true* story."

"Really? How can you be so sure?"

"Because giants aren't real, are they? Only Vikings believe in giants."

Edmund opens his mouth to reply, but it's my turn to test him now – and I think I can get him wriggling like an eel on a spike.

"Besides," I say casually, "everyone knows that Keku the Frog created the marshes."

I have to force myself not to laugh at the stunned expression on his face. He wasn't expecting that! "A frog?!"

"You know the story of Keku the Frog, right?"

"Kek... Who? Keku? The Frog. Of course. Well, why don't you remind me?"

KEKU THE FROG

A long time ago – way before words like "long", "time" and "ago" were invented – a frog lived in the Fens. Normal grassy fields – that's what the Fens were back then.

Now there's one thing you need to understand at the start of this story: back then, frogs looked a lot like you and me. They stood upright on two straight legs, and had two arms, a body, and a head – all in the right places.

There were only two differences. One, their skin was green – though you can make yourself that colour if you eat nothing but mouldy bread for a week. And two, their eyes were on the sides of their heads – which is where your eyes end up if you watch a butterfly flying for too long. At least, that's what Dad says.

Anyway. The frog in this story was called Keku, and he was the Most Important Frog. He had been given a special job by Great Hunter Woden, the leader of all the sky gods: Keku had to decide if the rain should be on or off.

To do this, Keku had a magical stick: put it in the ground, and it rained; take it out, and the rain would stop.

All day every day, Keku stood in the middle of the Fens and studied the fields. If he reckoned they needed more water for things to grow, he put his stick in the ground – and *ffffsssshhhh!*

But as soon as the fields were watered enough, he took his stick *out* of the ground – and *shtp!*

Now, a river happened to pass near the spot where Keku would stand, and the fish swimming in the river loved to tease Keku. They'd say things like,

"Hey, have you heard? The sky gods are having a big party down at the beach! Why aren't you going? Oh yeah – you've got to stay with your special stick!"

But Keku just tried to ignore them. He was really proud of his job, and didn't care what anyone else thought.

Until one day...

Keku saw that the Fens needed some water, so he put his stick in the ground – and *ffffssssshhhh!*

As he looked downriver, he suddenly noticed a bright glow in the distance. It was a magnificent colour that Keku had never seen before. Beautiful. Enchanting. *Captivating.*

A fly flew in and out of his mouth, and Keku realised he'd been gawping at the strange glow for ages. Just then, he spotted some fish swimming from the direction of the glow – so he asked them what it was.

But the fish just laughed.

"If you want to know, you'll have to find out for yourself... you big green bogey with legs!"

That was the last straw. Keku had watered the Fens for a long time, and taken his job very seriously – but now he wanted to do something for himself. Besides, it didn't look very far away. Keku could just pop over, see what it was, then come back again. What'd be the harm in that?

So off he went, taking long strides through the rain until he was close enough to see what was causing the glow.

What he found was a long, flat boat – and, in that boat, sat a huge box full of *gold*.

Of course, Keku didn't know it was gold. He'd never seen gold before. But he did know two things. One, it was beautiful. And two, he *wanted* it.

So he stepped into the boat and put his arms around the box. Crumbs – it was super heavy! But Keku knew the best way to lift heavy things: he bent his knees as far down as they would go, hugged the box tight to his chest, then pushed his legs and tried to stand up.

But – *eeeff!* The box was so massively heavy! Keku did manage to get it off the bottom of the boat – but only just! He staggered out of the boat, his knees still bent as he struggled to haul the precious box onto the land.

He made it! He panted from the effort. But then he noticed his feet sinking a little into the mud beneath the grass... He'd left the stick in the ground, so it was still raining – and now the fields were starting to flood!

Still, Keku wanted that gold. So he didn't put it down. Instead, he wheezed and grunted as he heaved his heavy load across the fields back to his special stick.

He kept his knees bent the whole way – partly to stop his back from breaking, and partly because the box was too heavy for him to get his legs straight! And the weight was so big that he couldn't move much faster than a snail. The rainwater soon crept up his knees... then his hips... then his belly-button...

But still Keku soldiered on. The marshes were flooding around him... but he wasn't giving up his treasure!

At last, after taking nearly the whole day, Keku reached the special stick – though he could barely see it, because the water was so high.

Just then, Great Hunter Woden swooped down from the sky. He grabbed the stick out from the ground, and the rain stopped straight away: *shtp!*

Angrily, Woden snatched the box away from Keku. Of course Keku felt guilty, and a little bit scared – but he was also relieved that the weight was gone. Finally he could stretch his legs...

But Woden pointed his magical finger at Keku's knees and boomed, "*No, Keku! The Fens are ruined because you were so greedy. I will punish you for* being so selfish. You will no longer have the special job of controlling the rain. And from now on, your legs will never be straight again!"

And that's why, if you see a frog today, you'll see they have bendy legs. As for the Fens, though – well, all that water seeped down into the fields, leaving the deep soggy marshes you can see all around the Fens today...

"See? *That's* how the marshes were *really* created!" I sit back down triumphantly.

"Fun story," says Edmund, flicking some dried mud off his leg wraps. "And of course it's so much easier to believe in a man-sized frog than in a giant."

That makes me smile, despite myself. "I know, it's silly, isn't it. But when my Mum tells that one, she..." I hear what I'm saying and bite my lip. "Never mind."

Edmund raises his eyebrows for a moment – but, thankfully, he wants to keep talking about my story. "There's another problem with your tale, of course."

"What's that, then?"

"It explains why the Fens are marshes, but it doesn't say why the land is flat. Mine did both."

I shrug. "It's just always been flat."

"Since when?"

"Since always!"

"Yes, but tell me a story to explain how it became so flat," insists Edmund.

"I don't know one!"

"Make one up, then! How would we know about Keku if nobody had ever wondered why marshes were marshy, then made up a story about it?"

I think about it... But my mind wanders, and I'm thinking about how Mum used to tell the story of Keku, and wishing I could ask her whether she made it up or whether someone else told her.

Maybe you can help me... Can *you* think of a story to explain how the Fens came to be so flat? If you can, write it over the next few pages – you can even add some pictures if you like...

One long Winter day a monkey lived
and the monkey worked for Wade. The gud
us the large large sea.

you see this monkey didn't really have
a name because his name was monkey
now this monky was special (not because of
his name) he was special because he was
all ways suppose to moving their marginal
sea orb the world keep the sea calm is
anyone else held the orb the sea will go
haywire. now here comes the real

story. One long Winter day the monky
was playing around and he uh uh uh dropped
the orb and uh uh scarce another monky
grabd the orb and the sea went haywire
and crazy and super CRAZEY!!!

The monkey quickly swung through
the trees while the other monkey
ran across the ..... a the waves
thrashed on the land and the monkey
running in the ..... rose.

the monkey ..... monkey ..... caught
up to the other monkey and then
..... the ..... to their side and
.... and made
the .... shut. ..... is .....
..... land .... have water
in it is the .... then they
..... and the ran ....
side ways and still ....
while ..... was ..... mental
thing.

Finally the monkey an got the erb and the end was calm aester that every one had a huge party and monkey was not invited to all because the monkey that stole the erb didnt get the erb.

THE

End

illustrated by Joshua David Finch

all rev authed

"Now *that* was a great story!" smiles Edmund.

"It was, wasn't it?" I say. "I wish I could tell it to Mum."

Edmund speaks really gently: "Ethelred... What's happened to your mum?"

He looks so kind and ready to listen... so it's a good thing Dad comes in and rescues me by plonking a huge pot of eel stew on the table and lifting the lid.

"His mum's gone," Dad says firmly. "That's the end of *that* story."

So I finish off the nearly normal evening trying not to laugh at Edmund's attempts to pretend he likes eel stew. Whatever he says, I can tell he's not really from round here.

But he seems friendly enough. And anyway – we all have secrets.

A Hill Outside the Window

The next morning, I wake up before anyone else. So I decide to go to the river and wash while no-one's about.

The water is clear and very cold, but at least I don't have to break the ice. The first splash stings with cold – but I remember washing with Mum and how she always used to say, "Don't scream! Either laugh or sing instead, then you'll make a joyful noise instead of a painful one!"

So I laugh. I remember last summer when she and I played in this bit of the river, pretending we were eels, and swimming to catch each others' toes under the water.

Then I remember how Mum loved to sing, and I

want to sing too. Mum taught me a beautiful ballad, full of longing...

But that's not how I want to feel right now. I want to be playful! So I think of Edmund's challenge from yesterday – making up a story to explain why the land is flat – and a silly idea for a new song pops into my head. I sing it out now, splashing the water of the river to help me keep the rhythm...

A hill outside the window
            was all a witch could see.
So with a magic clap,
The hill went flat,
And now outside her eye could spy
            A cow: **"Moooo!"**
And another...

...hill outside the window
            was all a witch could see.
So with a magic clap,
The hill went flat,
And now outside her eye could spy
            A cow: **"Moooo!"**
            And a pig: **"Oink oink!"**
And another...

...hill outside the window
           was all a witch could see.
So with a magic clap,
The hill went flat,
And now outside her eye could spy
           A cow: **"Moooo!"**
           And a pig: **"Oink oink!"**
           And a duck: **"Quack quack!"**
           And another...

...hill outside the window
           was all a witch could see.
So with a magic clap,
The hill went flat,
And now outside her eye could spy
           A cow: **"Moooo!"**
           And a pig: **"Oink oink!"**
           And a duck: **"Quack quack!"**
And...
           ...the beautiful blue and watery salty sea!

By the time I realise that Edmund is standing behind me, it's too late. I scramble to the bank and make a grab for my cloak, but he's seen and he's heard, and I know that he knows.

He knows that I'm not really a boy.

Secrets

"Ethelred!" wheezes Edmund from the place where I've got him pinned, flat on his back in the mudbank, my foot keeping him there, the eel spear held very close to his neck. "It's only me!"

I'm glad I carried the spear with me, just in case. "I can see that it's you," I respond coldly.

"And I can see you have a big secret," he says,

"but I won't tell anyone. You can trust me."

"How can I be sure?"

"Because I'm good at keeping secrets. I have a big secret, too. How about I tell you *my* secret? Then we'll have to trust each other."

"What is it?" I say warily.

"Can I get up and show you?"

I'm expecting him to reveal that he's not really an English man, and I'm ready with my response of, "Well, duh". I'm not sure it's worth taking my spear away from his neck for that information.

Still, I release him cautiously – but I remain ready to pounce as he reaches into the bag he's carrying...

My jaw drops when he pulls out a shining crown, glinting with precious metals, and presses it down over his mud-covered hair.

I look around on both sides, wondering whether Dad's up yet and how quickly someone would come if I really screamed.

"Oh my word... You're a thief?! You've stolen the king's crown?!"

At this, he laughs cheerfully. "No, silly – I *am* the king!"

He throws back his head, puts his hands on his hips, and peers down at me. His mock regal stature looks all the more comical as a chunk of mud falls off his elbow and splats to the ground.

"I am King Knut – king of all the Vikings and the English."

No – he can't be. He looks nothing like an ogre. But his voice definitely sounds like a king's voice. And that's definitely a crown on his head. *And* he didn't try stealing anything from us yesterday – meaning he's probably not a thief.

So now I can't help wondering whether I've really just had four spikes pointed towards a Viking king's windpipe – and let him go. "But why... if... who..."

I take a deep breath and start again.

"If that's true, what are you doing here pretending to be a normal English man?"

"Ah." He settles himself on a log and pats the space beside him for me to join him. "If this treaty of secrets is going to become more binding, I expect the same of your side of the bargain."

"Meaning?" I perch right at the other end of the log.

"If I tell you why I pretended to be a normal English man, will you tell me why you were pretending to be a boy yesterday?"

I look into his eyes, and his gaze is steady, his face kind under the crown which glows gold in the new morning light. "I suppose so," I say.

"Very well. But if we're going to trust each other, I need to know your real name. I know you're not Ethelred."

"I'm just Ethel."

"Hello, Ethel, nice to meet you... properly."

He smiles, and holds his hand out along the space. I inch very slightly closer, just enough to stop myself falling off the end of the log, and shake his hand by the tips of his fingers.

"Hello, King Knut. Nice to meet you properly too."

"Right then, are you sitting comfortably? I'll tell you why I'm dressed as an Anglo-Saxon. It all started when I was about your age, Ethel – but it's a... not very nice story, I'm afraid."

A Not Very Nice Story

When I was a boy, one of my favourite people was my aunt Gunhilda. I loved going to stay with her. She lived in a big house by the sea, on the east coast of the kingdom of Mercia*, and she used to tell me all the wonderful Viking sagas and histories.

---

* This would have been in the area that we now call the East Midlands, somewhere near Hull.

Aunt Gunhilda was my father's sister, and the three of us used to spend lots of time together.

Then once, when we were staying at her house, a battle started on the beach.

Being the King of Denmark, my father immediately left to fight. It turned out that the King of all the English and the Vikings, who was an English one at the time, had decided to get rid of all the Vikings – not just the soldiers, but the innocent people going about their everyday lives. And that included Viking women.

We were used to armies fighting for land, but this was different.

My father and some other men tried to hold the English back on the beach, but there were too many of them. They burst into the town and destroyed everything that so much as reminded them of a Viking.

Aunt Gunhilda got me to help her push furniture against the door of her house to stop them from getting in. That seemed to work – but I felt I should be doing more.

I wanted to go and fight alongside my father. So I kissed my aunt goodbye, climbed out of a window, and ran up to the top of a cliff to see if I could spot

my dad.

I couldn't see him anywhere – but the English soldiers had moved along the beach, and our Viking soldiers were battling them in the distance. It seemed to be going well. So I looked back down into the town.

But I couldn't see my aunt's house anymore.

It was behind a cloud of smoke. The English had set the small Viking village on fire. Including the house where I'd left my aunt.

I never saw Aunt Gunhilda again. I did find my father, and I joined the battle – and, as I'm sure you know, eventually we won. But it didn't matter how many English kingdoms we took over – it never brought my aunt back.

When I became the king of all the English and the Vikings, I knew that I had to stop the same thing happening again. We have to find a way to live peacefully together in this land – and, to do that, I must find out what English people need to be happy.

It's no good asking the English, because they'll just tell me that they want the Vikings to go home. But that's not possible any longer – too many families have lived here for too long. And it wouldn't stop the fighting anyway – we'd all just hate each other across the sea.

So no. I have to work out what the English really need to live peacefully alongside the Vikings. And that's why I decided to disguise myself as an everyday English man – to talk to some everyday English people.

King Knut finishes his story with, "So that's what I've been doing here – getting to know some of the English, and working out what they really need."

"What have you discovered so far?" I ask.

He smiles kindly. "That there are some really friendly English people out there. Like your dad."

I snort a bit too loudly. "You think my dad is friendly?! Even *I* think he looks grumpy all the time!"

"Maybe he doesn't smile much," agrees the king, "but think about last night. Even though he was obviously suspicious of me and didn't know who I was, he still let me in so I wouldn't drown in the marshes. He even shared your meal with me."

"I suppose so," I say. My dad? 'Friendly'? It's a day full of surprises so far.

"Anyway: your turn," says Knut. "You've heard my story, Ethel, so now: tell me yours. Why were you 'Ethelred' when I turned up yesterday? Why were you pretending to be a boy?"

It's the bit I've been dreading. "Mine's *another* not very nice story, I'm afraid..."

Another Not Very Nice Story

We were so happy, Mum and Dad and me, living in our little house by the river. The Fens may seem cold, flat and unfriendly to a stranger, but to us they've always been home. Dad taught me to catch eels, and Mum taught me all about the insects, birds, fish and flowers that live here. Mum also told me stories and made me laugh. Sometimes she even managed to make Dad laugh too.

That was before the monks came along. They built a new Abbey and moved in. Usually monks are busy, helpful people. They either spend their time praying, or do good works like building, farming and looking after sick people. So at first we were really happy that we'd have an Abbey nearby.

But these monks were different. They never went outside the Abbey. They were fat and lazy and greedy.

Soon they were so lazy that they didn't want to do anything for themselves. So they started kidnapping women to do all the work for them. Peoples' mums and daughters started disappearing from the fields and the rivers and even from their own front gardens. Once they'd been dragged into the Abbey, nobody saw them again.

The day they took Mum away, we were washing clothes by the river together. I went to hang my tunic up to dry, and when I turned round I saw three monks sneaking up on Mum from the reeds.

I was too scared to shout because I knew they'd take me as well – and they were so quick that I couldn't think of any way to help her. One put his fat hand over her mouth, the other two lifted her

up, and they were gone.

I crouched down in the reeds and hid. I can't believe I let them take her like that. But what else *could* I have done?

When I got home and told Dad what had happened, he was worried they would come back for me – so he disguised me as a boy to keep me safe. I've been Ethelred ever since.

And that's why I got up so early this morning. It's safer to be outside before dawn, because the monks are probably still asleep.

MAKING A PLAN

"That's dreadful!"

Knut leaps from the log like a toad when you surprise it from behind.

"Where are these monks? They need to be taught a lesson! How dare they behave like that? Monks are supposed to be Christians! Christians don't kidnap women and make them do horrible jobs around the house!"

He's waving his arms around, and trying to stride impressively to and fro (which isn't really working as he's sinking up to his knees in mud with every step). Frustrated, he turns to me and holds out his hand.

"How do you live in this ridiculous place?! Get me out of this marsh, quickly! There's no time to lose!"

I pull him back up from the riverbank as I ask, "Why, where are we going?"

"Where are we going? We're going to sort those monks out once and for all! We're going to kick their fat backsides from here to Ragnarok!*

"But to start with, we're going back to your house, Ethel. We need to tell your father the truth about who I am – and we need to make a plan..."

*   *   *

When Knut and I walk into my house looking very much like ourselves, Dad starts flapping about like a freshly caught eel. He looks from me to Knut and back to me again.

"You! Boy! Ethel! Girl! Him! Crown! Hide...!"

It's clear he's not going to stop any time soon.

---

* 'Kingdom come' in Viking language.

Knut makes a few attempts to explain, but Dad doesn't let him get much further than "Li–", "Loo–", "Pl–".

So, at last, Knut strides over and slaps his face. "Calm down, good man, I'm not going to hurt you!"

"Ow!" says Dad.

But, at last, he's listening. So, before he can start panicking again, Knut and I quickly try to tell Dad everything we've found out about one another. At first it doesn't go well at all because we keep starting to speak at exactly the same time – and then we each stop to let the other one go first.

Eventually, though, Knut puts one hand over his own mouth and points to me with his other hand.

"Dad, it's all going to be fine!" I explain. "This is not really an English man called Edmund. It's a Viking called– *CALM DOWN!*"

Dad's grabbed the eel spear. I quickly step between him and the king.

"He's a *friendly* Viking, Dad. And he's also – get this, Dad – he's also... the King! This is King Knut!"

Dad stares at Knut.

Knut nods and straightens his crown.

Dad stammers. "King Knut? The Viking king?"

That makes me giggle. "*Viking king...!*" They ignore me.

Dad is now talking to Knut. "What are you doing here?"

"Well, I was hiking in the marshes…"

I've really got the giggles now. *The Viking king hiking!"*

Dad frowns. "Whatever for? Do you like to hike?"
"Like to hike!"

Knut explains grandly: "I was hiking in disguise to find out about the English, and to extend a hand of friendship."

Dad scowls at Knut's extended hand of friendship for a moment – then, slowly and cautiously, he shakes it.

It's a serious, solemn moment – my dad, as English a man as any English man, shaking hands with one of our sworn enemies: King Knut, as Viking a man as any Viking. It's the first glimmer of peace between our two warring nations.

But I can't stop myself from guffawing.

"Perhaps you should have taken a bike! Or a trike! And carried a pointy stick to hit and poke people with!"

Now they're both staring at me.

Dad is frowning again. "Bikes haven't been invented yet," he points out.

Knut looks confused too. "Why would I have

wanted to do that?"

I take a deep breath. "Because then you would have been a biking, spiking, striking Viking King who likes to hike!"

I wheeze, wiping my eyes.

Dad looks at me for a few moments, then turns back to Knut. "What have you done to my daughter, King of the Vikings?"

"I'm king of the English too, you know," Knut corrects him, before crouching on one knee to help me up. "Do you need a drink of water, Ethel?"

"Now hang on a minute!" Dad interrupts. "A lot of English men have died because of Vikings like you. You'll never be the king of me."

Knut sighs, and I wonder whether he's thinking of his Aunt as he replies.

"A lot of Vikings have died too, Legres. I want the troubles to stop just as much as you do, and I'm doing my best to find a way to live peacefully. But while I'm working on that, we've got something else to sort out – I want to teach a lesson to those monks who stole your wife!"

Dad gasps, then glares at me. "You told him about your mother?"

"Of course!" I say happily. "He's the king, Dad, he can help us! He can march right in there and arrest all those fat, lazy, horrible monks!"

Dad puts his hand on my shoulder. "Oh, my poor Ethel. No, he can't."

"He can so!"

Knut is behind me. "No, I can't."

"Yes he ca– ...What?"

I turn to face Knut, who is shaking his head.

"Your dad's right, Ethel. I can't just go marching in. If the monks saw me coming, they'd cover their tracks, wouldn't they? They'd run away and hide all the evidence."

Dad suddenly sounds very grim indeed. "And your mother is evidence, Ethel. They might hide her from us – forever."

"But you said you wanted to teach them a lesson!" I realise I'm shouting.

Knut's voice, though, stays steady. "And I will. But to make sure that none of the women and girls are hurt, and to show that I am a fair and just king, we will have to be clever with how we go about it."

"Catch 'em red-handed!" growls Dad. "But how?"

Knut sounds more kingly than ever. "I think we'll need some help. Ethel, Legres... Do you have a boat? We must journey upriver, as quickly as we can."

Dad replies, "Of course we have a boat. Where are we going?"

"To Ely, where my Viking army are waiting for me with the monks of Saint Etheldreda's Shrine."

Dad shudders. "I don't trust Vikings."

I shudder too. "I don't trust monks."

But Knut is resolute – and the rhyme doesn't make me giggle this time.

"I didn't trust English men until now. But this time, we must all trust each other. Are you with me?"

We nod.

Knut smiles again. "Then let's go!"

To Ely

Knut settles himself gingerly on the seat of our narrow wooden barge, then looks up at Dad. "Your daughter has a beautiful voice, Legres. That's how I found her this morning – I followed the music. I thought perhaps the river was enchanted."

Dad plunges a long pole into the water and pushes the boat away from the bank. "She shouldn't have been singing," he replies gruffly. "Anyone could have heard you, Ethel."

I look at my feet.

Then Dad mutters, more softly, "Gets it from her mum."

"Well," says the king, "surely it's safe for her to

sing now? There's no-one around for miles, and she's got her dad and her king with her. So go on, Ethel: give us a song for our journey."

"Absolutely no," I say, "no way." To make my point extra clear, I take a big bite of the eel sandwich Dad packed for me.

"But why not?" whines Knut, sticking out his lower lip.

Honestly – what a big baby.

"I don't sing for *people*," I say, spraying him with crumbs.

"What shall we do to pass the time, then? More stories?"

"I don't want to tell stories," I say. "We're supposed to be working out how to rescue Mum. We should be planning. I was thinking you could besiege the abbey – those fat monks would come out pretty quickly to get food, and then–"

Dad interrupts, his voice flat. "They'd stop feeding your mum first."

"Oh. Right. Well, how about if you cover your soldiers in leaves and tell them to pretend to be bushes, then they can creep to the door so slowly the monks won't notice, and then–"

Knut interrupts this time. "Let me tell you about Etheldreda, whose shrine we're going to. Once, when she was running away from–"

I interrupt him right back.

"I know all about Etheldreda. Mum named me after her, didn't she? And hey, *Etheldreda* wouldn't think my idea was silly. Once, so that she wouldn't have to get married, she hid under a tree that grew straight out of her walking stick when she planted it in the ground."

Knut smiles. "Just what I was going to say! Your mother named you well, Ethel. You are just as resourceful as your namesake."

Dad grunts as he punts the boat along. "Shares a stubborn streak with her, too."

We float along in silence for a bit after that. I lean on the edge of the boat to watch a cormorant dive, and try to guess where its little black hook of a head will pop up next.

Then, out of nowhere, the sound of chanting voices comes creeping up like a mist from the ground.

"What's that?" I ask, pulling my arms back inside the boat.

King Knut points across the marsh, ahead of our boat.

"That's the monks at Saint Etheldreda's Shrine! We're getting close. Isn't their singing wonderful?"

I look to where he's pointing – I can see a slight hill rising, and the great grey buildings of a monastery and church.

Suddenly, Knut bursts out with a little song of his own:

> *Merry sing the monks in Ely*
> *As Knut the King goes passing by...*
> *Stop here, my friend, near the land,*
> *And let us listen to their song.*

He looks at me, chuffed as a chaffinch with the first worm of the day. "See? I can make up songs too."

I shrug. "It didn't rhyme."

As Dad guides the boat towards the bank, a boy with a bucket scrambles down the slope to the riverside. When he sees us, he starts waving furiously. I wave back, then feel stupid when I realise it's Knut he's waving to.

"Uncle!" he shouts as soon as he's close enough. "I didn't know you were coming back so soon!"

Knut grins, returning the wave. "Hello, Harald! I'm back on a special mission with my friends here. This is Legres, an eel catcher; and this is Ethel, his daughter. You two, this is my nephew Harald who's been travelling with my army – learning to fight."

"Hello," says Harald, and sticks out his hand. I take it, thinking he wants to shake hands, but it turns out that his plan was to help me out of the boat – with the result that he pulls me face forward into his chest and then backs off, apologising. I scowl at him.

Knut rescues him. "Harald, go and tell the others to be ready to receive us. We shall be wanting everyone's help."

The boy doesn't want telling again: he turns and runs, slipping twice as he climbs the hill at speed, dropping his bucket. It rolls back down, so I pick it up and fill it with water.

Then the three of us follow the sound of chanting up the hill to Saint Etheldreda's Shrine.

MONKS AND VIKINGS
AREN'T BEST FRIENDS

The room is full of people. Half the Viking soldiers seem to have brought their families with them, because there are men and women and children and dogs all over the place, all talking at once – well, not the dogs, but they're adding to the racket with barks and howls.

If you look at the level of everyone's heads (which is hard for me to do from down here), you can tell the monks by their bald patches, glinting in the candlelight. They are weaving in and out of the crowd, carrying plates of food and trying to encourage everyone to sit down, but it's a hopeless task. Knut explained what we were doing here about

half an hour ago, and nobody has stopped arguing since.

A Viking with a big red beard, and a louder voice than the rest, shouts out: "Why should we help the English? Weren't we killing them not long ago?"

A gaggle of Vikings in the corner raise their tankards of ale and yell in agreement: "Hear, hear!"

A nearby monk mildly suggests, "If you won't do it for the English, you could do it for us, your hosts..."

"We don't owe you anything!" growls Red Beard.

"That's rich!" spits a second, braver monk. "Don't owe us anything?! Barely a century ago, you lot were burning this place to the ground, and now look at you! Using us as a holiday inn!"

Mild Monk taps the arm of Brave Monk. "Forgiveness, brother."

From the look on Brave Monk's face, I wonder if he's forgotten what forgiveness means.

I tug on Knut's sleeve. "Is that true? The Vikings burnt the monastery?"

"About a hundred years ago, yes, but that's water under the bridge," he says impatiently. "Ethel, if I can't manage to make this lot stop squabbling, how am I ever going to make peace in the entire land?"

Knut looks back to the rest of the room, waves his arms, and yells: "*BE QUIET!*" But no-one can hear him.

He turns to me with a desperate look. "Ethel, can *you* do something?"

"Me?! What am *I* supposed to do?"

His answer seems to bring all the eels in my stomach back to life: "Sing to them! Your high voice will carry over all their low ones."

I try not to throw up. "I thought I made it clear on the boat: I don't sing for *people*."

"Don't sing for them, then. Sing for the land, just as you did when I found you."

Before I can protest any more, his strong arms wrap around me and hoist me up until I'm standing on a stool.

I want to be anywhere else. But Knut is smiling at me, reassuring – like he knows more about me than I do, and what he knows means that everything will be just fine.

"Just shut your eyes, Ethel," he whispers, "and imagine you're there by the river."

So I shut my eyes and think, about the river and the reeds and the sunrise.

And I start to sing...

We sailed across the seas,
Under rain and over foam –
Well, come hear the story
How the English found their home.

We found a land of green,
All around it we did roam –
Well, come hear the story
How the English found their home.

We all found our own corners,
Tried to build our homes alone –
But when wicked men came for us
We were overthrown...

But although they take our gold,
We will live another day.
We built seven kingdoms
And in seven kingdoms we shall stay.

I finish. I breathe. And then I realise:

Everyone's gone quiet.

When I open my eyes, a hundred pairs of eyes are looking back. One of the monks wipes a sleeve across his face. Across the room I can see Knut's nephew Harald staring at me with his mouth slightly open.

I grab my chance before everyone goes back to yelling. "Please, could you lot all listen to the king for a moment? He's *your* king, after all."

"Thank you, Ethel." Knut stands to address the room. "My people – for, as Ethel points out, you are all my people, Viking and English alike – it's time to stop thinking about our differences and unite where we agree. We can all agree that what has happened to Ethel's mother is wrong – so why can't we all fight it together, instead of fighting each other? In fact–"

He pauses as an idea pops into his head.

"In fact, Ethel's beautiful song has given me an idea. She was singing for the land. It's our land, all of ours, and it's a great land. Can't we fight together for this land, instead of fighting each other *over* it?"

"Hear, hear!" shout the Vikings with the tankards.

"Hear, hear!" cries the Brave Monk.

Then Red Beard adds his "Hear, hear!"... then Mild Monk adds *his* "Hear, hear,"... and then they're *all* doing it! Yelling in agreement and clinking their tankards.

And somehow, even through all that excited noise, I hear another voice – tiny in comparison, but still full of enthusiasm. It's Knut's nephew, Harald, who's punching the air.

"Yeah!" he calls out. "Go Uncle Knut!"

I nearly jump out of my skin as Dad tugs my sleeve. And, for a moment, I wonder if he's ill – because, for the first time *ever*, he's smiling.

"Go Ethel," he says.

Naming the Land

(well, kinda...)

It's stupid Brave Monk who starts it. At the top of his voice, he blurts out, "Hear, hear for our land – the land of East Anglia!"

Half the joy seems to fly out the windows as all the Vikings go quiet. A few of the monks cheerily cry, "Hear, hear!" – but then they realise what's happened, and they too shut up.

Then that brute with the red beard stands straighter, and I hunch my shoulders – as do most of the monks – as we expect him to bellow some angry reply.

But actually, Red Beard just calls over to Knut.

"Your Majesty – my home is in Northumbria. East Anglia isn't my land at all."

Knut's still smiling, but I'm close enough to see how he grinds his teeth a little before answering. "You have Viking brothers who live here in East Anglia. It's as much your land as it is theirs, and it's as much theirs as it is the monks."

But then another Viking pipes up, one who seems to like wearing his helmet indoors: "I don't have Viking brothers in East Anglia *or* Northumbria. I joined your army in Mercia."

And another, who must have lost half his nose in a battle once: "Nme too! I joinned your armny inn *Dennmark*! All nmy brothers are back there! Apart fromn onne. He's inn Nnorway..."

Mild Monk weighs in: "I just popped up from Wessex to say hello to my old Latin teacher. I don't have any family here either."

Half-nose is still going. "Annd nmy sister. She's inn Swedenn..."

Knut sighs. "I didn't mean *actual* brothers. I meant brothers in... brothers in..."

I squint, not sure if I'm being helpful as I say, "Brothers in land?"

"Yes!" declares Knut. "Brothers in land!"

But everyone else in the room just looks puzzled.

Clearly I wasn't very helpful after all.

Knut is more confident, though. He's realised he still has everyone's attention, and he's not going to lose it.

"My people, what do all your lands have in common? *Me!* I am your king – king of all the English and the Vikings. So don't think of yourselves as coming from seven different English kingdoms, or three Viking ones. From now on, all the land I rule on this island is one. And any man who lives here now – English or Viking, wherever they're from – shall be a man of this land! The land of... of..."

He looks down at me again, and it gradually dawns on me that he's expecting me to come up with the perfect idea again.

But come up with the name of a whole new *kingdom?*

I simply can't think. I shrug, mouthing the word, "Sorry!"

Brave Monk shoots off again: "Call it East Anglia! You had the idea here, Your Majesty, so it's only fair."

To my surprise, it's another monk who replies to him: "He can't call the *whole* of it East Anglia, you twit! Some of it's in the north, south and west!"

"Mightyland!" That comes from Helmet Indoors.

"Peaceland!" That comes from Mild Monk.

"Redland!" That comes from... Well, duh.

Suddenly Half-Nose starts hopping about excitedly. "I knnow! I knnow! I've ngot it! *Knnutlannd!*"

A few Vikings cheer at this, but many of the monks mumble. Knut throws up his hands. "Knutland is a lovely suggestion, Oskar. But let's not forget – we haven't made friends with all the English men on this island yet. They might not take kindly to their land being named after the leader who just beat them in battle...

"My people – this is what we should do. All of us, as we sleep tonight, should try to think of the best name for the new kingdom we have made by bringing all seven English kingdoms together. If you have a good idea, carve it on a tablet and pass it to me – but only *after* we have dealt with those wicked monks who stole Ethel's mother.

"For now, all of you: get some much-needed rest!"

This time, everyone cheers at the same time: "Hear, hear!"

One Big Problem

Everyone else is leaving. Dad is looking at Knut with an expression I've never seen on his face before. I think it's... admiration?

"Those were some good strong speeches there," Dad tells Knut. "Not bad."

But Knut sighs. "Thank you, Legres. However, I did fail to achieve what I actually wanted from this gathering of our friendly monks and soldiers: we didn't discuss how we're going to get your wife back from those monks."

Just then, we're approached by a stooping, hook-nosed old monk. He's wearing the same habit that all the other monks are wearing, but he also has a really large cross hanging from a chain around his neck and covering the middle of his chest.

He's clearly an important monk, and his voice sounds like a candle flame: flickering, but bright and warm. "My name is Alfsig, and I am the Abbot here. We are at your service, Your Majesty, but may I first make a plea for my brothers? I can scarcely believe that an Abbot like myself would lead his monks so far wrong. Let us not punish them before we have proof."

I nearly explode. "We do have proof! My mum's the proof, and I saw what happened with my own eyes!"

Dad lays a hand on my arm to calm me down, but then he clears his throat. "Forgive my daughter, Father Abbot, but she's right. We are here as witnesses. If we're not going to be believed, we'll go home again."

"Stay where you are, Legres," says Knut. "Father Abbot needs proof for the same reason I do – to show the rest of the world that we are just and fair leaders, and that we are keeping peace in the land – not just starting war.

"Remember: if this looks like just another Viking army deciding to burn down a monastery, then your story will never be believed, and things will never change. Besides, remember what you said yourself earlier: for the safety of your wife, we *must* catch them red-handed."

Dad shakes his head. "But how? Like *you* said earlier: if they see you coming, they'll hide the evidence before you get there."

Knut pats Dad on the arm. "It certainly is one big problem. But don't worry, Legres: you get some rest. You've earned it after all your punting on the river today." Then he looks at me. "Ethel and I will work out how to get inside the abbey."

I blink. "We will?"

*   *   *

Abbot Alfsig takes Knut and me to a nook near the fire, where there's a table and some stools. Knut offers one to me, then he sits on the stool opposite.

As Alfsig bows and leaves, I'm still somewhat stunned. "Why are you talking about this with me? Shouldn't you be making plans with your cleverest Viking soldiers?"

Knut shakes his head. "Viking soldiers are clever at working out how to barge into an abbey. But *sneaking* into an abbey? That requires a different kind of clever. And I see that kind of clever in you, Ethel."

"You do?"

"Yes. You were right earlier, when you spoke about Saint Etheldreda's miraculous hiding places. That's what we need – a way to see inside the abbey without being seen ourselves."

I let one hand fall heavily on the table. "So what are you suggesting? That we pray for a miracle?"

There's that glimmer in Knut's eyes again. "It wouldn't be the first miracle to start with the action of a child. Have you heard the one about the bread and the fish?"

All I can think of is my sandwich from earlier. "Bread and fish?"

"Ask Abbot Alfsig to tell you later. Right now, though, we need to think... How could we see what's going on in that abbey without being seen?"

I hunch over the table, desperately searching my mind for an idea. Across from me, Knut does the same.

But an idea pops into my head first. "Maybe *another* story could help us."

Knut looks curious. "Go on...?"

I lick my lips, then begin. "Well, Mum told me lots of good ones about Woden, the Great Hunter who was the leader of the sky gods. He had to sneak around sometimes – like the time he needed to get back the potion of poetry..."

THE POTION OF POETRY

One day, Great Hunter Woden gathered all gods in his hall among the clouds, and declared:

"Friends! It is time we invented stories!"

Woden's wife, Frige, asked, "Why?"

He grinned at her. "So everyone can hear about our amazing adventures, of course!"

But Woden's son Thunor asked, "What's a story?"

So Woden told him. "It's a mixture of creativity, memory, cleverness and planning."

Thunor gasped. "That's a mixture of everything us gods do!"

"Exactly!" said Woden. "Inventing stories will need a little bit of all of us. That's why I've brought this bucket: we all need to spit in it!"

So they did. And because gods are as big as giants, they soon had a *huge* amount of spit.

You may think that's disgusting. And it was. But Woden added some honey, stirred it up, and poured it into three golden jugs.

Then he told everyone, "By tomorrow, this mixture of god spit and honey will have made a potion. Anyone who drinks it will be able to create stories in all sorts of ways: music, poetry, dance... maybe one day writing, television and computer games too, once those things have been invented!"

The gods went to bed excited, looking forward to drinking the potion in the morning. But that night, two trolls broke into Woden's hall, hoping to steal something pretty – like a gold jug.

Have you ever seen a troll? Their skin is yellow like earwax, hairy like a dog's bottom, and smelly like a boot that hasn't been taken off for six whole weeks. These two were called Stinker and Bogie.

Stinker found the gold jugs first, and peered inside. "Ey, Bogie! It smells like da gods spitted in 'ere!"

Bogie came over, his eyes wide. "Oo! Wha'sit taste like?"

Stinker scooped out a dollop of potion with his finger, and sucked it. "Tastes a bit like *honey*. But – oo, I *do feel funny*..."

Bogie scratched his nose. "Ey, Stinker. You just said 'honey' and then said 'funny'. That were odd."

Stinker rolled around for a bit, clutching his tummy, then his throat, and finally his head. Eventually he stopped, stood up, and said,

I feel as clever as a god!
It seems I've drunk a magic drink
So now I have the power to think,
Create, remember, plot and scheme –
These skills are every bad guy's dream!

Bogie was amazed. "Dat's great, brother. Can I 'ave some?"

But Stinker shook his head.

No! You can't! You're far too dumb!
I'm the oldest, and I'm the worst –
Besides all that, I found them first.
These golden jugs, one two and three,
From this day on belong to me!

Bogie scratched his head. "Ey, Stinker. I said 'some' and you said 'dumb'. Dat were weird."
Stinker rolled his eyes.

Not as weird as your wonky green beard!

Bogie scratched his chin. "Ey, Stinker. I said 'weird' and you said 'beard'. Dat were strange."
Stinker put his hands on his hips.

*I'll **yank** your beard if this subject won't change!*

Bogie scratched his cheek. "Ey, Stinker. I said 'strange' and you said 'change'. Do you fink you'll rhyme wiv everyfink I say?"
Stinker sighed.

It's looking as if it will be that way.
Now hush your nonsense, and give me a hand
Hiding these jugs deep down in the land!

Later, when the gods woke up, they were all shocked to find the potion was gone!

Woden commanded everyone, "Search the land! Our potion must be found!"

Woden himself began looking around for the lost potion. He didn't stop for three days. At the end of those days, though, he was near some big hills when he noticed a yellowish log with some green moss growing at the end of it. So he decided to sit and rest.

"Oy! Gerroff!"

Woden stood and looked down. It seemed he had just sat on a sleeping troll.

Straight away, Woden knew something wasn't right. Trolls normally slept in caves or under bridges – not next to big hills. He also knew trolls liked stealing things. *And* he knew trolls wouldn't be completely honest with sky gods.

But he also knew trolls could be pretty stupid. So he started by saying, "Oh, sorry. I didn't see you there. What's your name?"

You've probably guessed the troll's name, haven't you? "Bogie."

"What are you doing here?"

"Nuffink."

Woden raised an eyebrow. "'Nuffink'? That's

what trolls say when they're trying to hide something, isn't it."

Bogie suddenly looked worried. "Is it? Oh. In dat case, I mean, sumfink."

Woden nodded. "I see. 'Sumfink' is what trolls say when they're hiding something nearby, isn't it."

Bogie bit his nails. "Is it? In dat case, I mean, anyfink."

"Right. 'Anyfink' is what trolls say when they're hiding something in a hill right next to them, isn't it."

Bogie whined. "Is it?! In dat case, I mean, everyfink!"

"Thank you!" replied Woden. "'Everyfink' is what trolls say when they want you to take a look inside the hill next to them, isn't it! Well then, I'd better take a look inside this one..."

"No!" Bogie jumped in Woden's way. "You can't do dat! Besides, dere's nuffink inside diss hill."

"Really? Then why won't you let me look inside it?"

"Coz... I'm trying to help you! I'm trying to stop you wasting your time."

Woden shrugged. "Oh, I won't mind. Digging into hills is a hobby of mine."

Now Bogie pulled a long blade out from the side of his shorts. "I can't let you..."

Woden quickly held up his hands. Normally he was strong enough to fight a troll, but he had just been walking around for three days non-stop – so he knew there was a chance he could get badly hurt. Plus, if you start fighting one troll, other trolls will soon come along. Woden didn't want to be outnumbered – especially when he didn't yet know if Bogie was guarding the potion of poetry.

So instead, Woden said, "Alright, alright. Just prove to me that the hill is empty, and I'll go. Drill a really small hole through the hill – all the way to the other side – and if I can blow through the hole, I'll know you're telling the truth."

Bogie's tiny little brain thought about this for a moment. If the hole was really small, he thought, it would be too dark for Woden to see anything. And Bogie was sure that Woden would be able to blow through any hole, even if it didn't go all the way to the other side.

So Bogie figured that Woden would be easily tricked into thinking the hill was empty, and used his blade to drill a small hole in the side of the hill.

It was about the width of your wrist – and of course it was very, very dark. After about a minute, Bogie stepped back. "Go on, den – blow!"

Woden blew into the hole... and loads of dust

came out! "The hill must be hiding something," he said, "otherwise there wouldn't be any dust! I'm going to get the rest of the sky gods..."

"Wait!" pleaded Bogie. "Maybe I din't drill far enuff. Let me keep going..."

Bogie drilled deeper for another minute, then invited Woden to take another blow. Once again, a cloud of dust burst out from the hillside.

"You're lying to me!" cried Woden. "I'm off to get the sky gods now..."

"No!" begged Bogie. "It must be just a little way more. Hold on..."

Bogie drilled even deeper for one more minute, then let Woden take another blow.

This time, there was no dust.

"See?" said Bogie, proudly. "I's drilled right froo de hill. Dere's nuffink inside."

Woden smiled. He knew Bogie *hadn't* drilled all the way through the hill – that would have taken ages. But if no dust was blowing out, that meant Bogie must have drilled into a secret lair inside the hill instead!

For now, though, Woden just said, "Thank you, Bogie. I believe you. I'll be on my way. Have a good day."

Woden walked away, until he had turned a

corner. He checked that Bogie couldn't see him – and then he put his arms by his sides, poked out his tongue, and said, "*Hissssssssss...*"

In a flash... he turned into a *snake!*

Bogie took no notice of the snake slithering towards that little hole he'd just drilled into the side of the hill. Instead, he sat on the grass, happily gazing at the clouds, looking forward to telling his brother about how he'd tricked the Great Hunter Woden.

Snake Woden slipped into the hole, wriggled through it, and soon popped out in an underground lair. In there was a girl troll (you could tell it was a girl troll, because it was slightly less hairy), and beside her were Woden's three golden jugs.

Snake Woden transformed back into Great Hunter Woden.

The girl troll screamed:

"*Daaaaaaaddeeeeeeeee...!*"

Woden held up his hand. "Silence! Do you know who I am?"

The troll shook her head.

"I am Great Hunter Woden, leader of the sky gods. Who are you?"

The troll bowed. "My name is Hilda. I'm the daughter of the troll called Stinker."

"These three golden jugs belong to me," Woden told her. "Do you know who stole them?"

The troll's cheeks went red. "Daddy did, with Uncle Bogie. Please, Mister Woden – I don't mean you no harm. But now I've called Daddy's name, he'll be here soon!"

Woden looked around him. "This secret lair must have a proper way out. Where is it?"

Hilda pointed up. "The top of the hill opens, but only when Daddy says the word: 'orange'."

Woden frowned. "That's a strange secret password."

"Daddy chose it because it only works when he says it. But because he drunk your potion, he has to rhyme with the last thing anyone has said – and Daddy believes nothing rhymes with 'orange'."

Woden thought really hard, but even he couldn't think of a single word that rhymed with 'orange'.

"Besides," continued Hilda, "Daddy needed Uncle Bogie's help to carry all three jugs away from your hall in the clouds. How would you carry them now? You've only got two hands!"

Woden's eyes flickered. "*That* is an easy one!"

In a flash, Woden turn into... a giant pelican! An enormous bird with a long beak, under which hung a great big sack! Pelican Woden flew to each of the jugs in turn and sucked the potion into that sack.

Just as he sucked up the last drop, though, the hill opened. In jumped Stinker, along with an army of about ten other trolls – and the hill closed above them.

All the trolls held long sharp blades. Stinker was at the front, grinning a toothy grin.

Welcome Woden, you fine ol' chap –
You've landed right here in my trap!
Now you'll meet my hungry troll clan...
Tonight we dine on fried pelican!

Woden gulped. Not because he was scared, though. He was actually swallowing just a little drop of the poetry potion...

And, as he did, an idea popped into his head. He said,

Alright Stinker, you win – I agree.
But can you answer one question for me?
What word will move your magic door hinge?

Stinker's face suddenly screwed up, like a cow pat melting in the sun. He bit his lip and held his breath – until, when he couldn't hold it any longer, he had to blurt out,

IT MOVES WHENEVER I UTTER 'ORANGE'!

Instantly, the hill opened again – and, like a bolt of lightning with feathers, Pelican Woden shot up and into the sky. Behind him came a furious roar... as Stinker watched Pelican Woden soar...

See how I rhymed that bit at the end?
That's 'cause Woden was everyone's friend.
He shared that potion with folks like you and me
So we can share tales, and music – and poetry.
And soon, of course, the world overflowed in
Stories about the Great Hunter Woden.

Disguises

As I finish, Knut has a cheeky smile on his face. "I can do lots of things, Ethel, but I don't think I can turn myself into a snake. And I know my double chin might *look* like the pouch under a pelican's beak, but I can't just sprout feathers and fly either."

I feel like I've just tripped and fallen flat in a puddle of thick mud. "Yeah. Sorry. It was stupid."

"What's stupid?"

The question comes from Harald, who steps brightly into the room with a tray of bread and cheese. "I thought you might need a snack – it's getting late."

Knut welcomes him. "Harald! Come and help us. We're trying to think of disguises – ways to get into the abbey without being seen."

"Oh, right!" Harald sets his tray down on the table and then fills his mouth with a bite of cheese. "Owa gout a nunk?"

I blink twice. "What?"

Harald swallows. "Sorry. How about a monk? We could borrow some habits from the brothers here."

Knut shakes his head. "Ah, dear nephew, we'd be caught out in an instant. Monks don't walk around with their hoods up all the time – and do you think our soldiers will be happy shaving off most of their hair to look like they have tonsures?* Besides, if the monks are behaving badly, will they really want to let in other monks to see how lazy they are?"

Undeterred, Harald pauses his next mouthful long enough to say, "How about lepers? We could wrap up in bandages and ask to go to their infirmary."

I snort at the mental image of Vikings wrapped head to toe in bandages. "That would be funny, but no – the monks aren't doing their jobs, remember? They're turning away sick people."

The conversation gets a bit silly after that, as we start imagining different disguises, and how we could make them. I ask you: what would *you* use to make these costumes? Write your ideas here:

---

* That's the bald patch in the middle of a monk's head.

An Anglo-Saxon Soldier

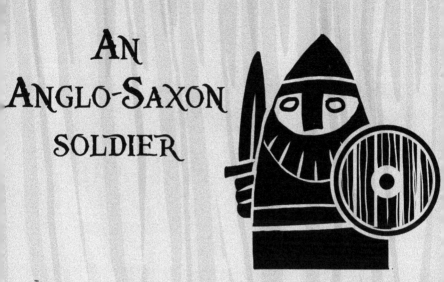

First get metal wood and gold for the helmet I would get a black is metal and move the inside out and make a move on top is the helmet and then add gold speckled around the helmet circle is metal then get a a thin metalic and much point ring and a small then put wood in side the metal ring and put the point on in the middle is the wood.

A HARE

get pink paper white fur and
make an oval with your
fur the cut two of them and
cut an an a bigger oval inside
one of the bigger ovals and
stick the full oval and the
pink paper (by the way the
pink paper needs to be in
a oval shape to) stick the full
oval and the pink paper together
and the cut oval over the
top of the pink paper and full
oval.

A FAIRY

get a house and 3 leaves
cut (get ribbon too) 2 leaves
'em a wing shape and get
you wings and ribbon and
put stick your ribbing on
your leaves and put your
3rd has circle it and cut
the bottom bit in a zigzag
shape.

A Troll

get wood and make it look like a club and paint it green and finally put a wig and %100 put

PERFECT

Harald picks up two pieces of the cheese rind, sticks them into his mouth to make fangs, and starts doing his best troll impression. I'm holding my sides laughing.

Knut guffaws – then gasps. "Oh! Oh, I've just remembered the *funniest* story about disguises! Have you heard about the time Thor lost his hammer?"

THOR'S STOLEN HAMMER

You must have heard of Thor, right? The god who made the sky echo with thunderous crashes from his mighty hammer? He was the prince of the gods, their strongest warrior, the chief guardian of Asgard where all the gods lived.

And, at the start of this story, he was having a *huge* strop.

"I can't do it! I *won't* do it! Everyone will laugh at me!"

He thumped the arm of his throne in anger – and one whole half of his throne promptly disintegrated. Thor slid out and landed in a heap on the marble floor of the palace hall.

Nearly every other god around the banquet table covered their mouths, pretending to cough or yawn, hoping that Thor wouldn't notice the giggles behind their fingers.

Only three gods didn't cover their faces. One was Loki. Of all the gods, Loki loved a good joke – so he just threw his head back and let out a huge laugh.

But Odin and Freya, the high king and queen of the gods, didn't cover their faces either. They weren't anywhere close to laughing.

Odin looked gravely at Thor. "My son – you must. If you don't, you won't have your greatest weapon when the great battle of Ragnarok comes."

Thor picked himself up off the floor, wiped the dust from his armour, folded his arms, and sulked – but he knew his father was right.

You see, Thor's hammer was called Mjollnir, which means "lightning". That's because, if you threw it at someone, it would shoot towards them as fast as light. It never missed. And it always flew back to Thor's hand like a superfast homing pigeon.

So of course Thor would need Mjollnir at Ragnarok, the big battle at the end of days. The books of the future all told that the gods would have a huge war with the giants – and they needed Mjollnir to win.

But, that morning, Thor and Loki found that Mjollnir had been stolen.

Thor immediately suspected a giant was to blame, so he sent Loki to search for it. Loki was a shapeshifter: he easily turned into a falcon and soared across the sky to Jotunheim – the land of the giants.

There, Loki found Mjollnir in the cave of the chief giant, Thrym. He flew to Thrym and told him to return the hammer, or else Thor would come and beat him up.

But Thrym knew Thor couldn't beat him in a fight without Mjollnir. He told Loki, "There's only one way Thor is getting his hammer back: if his mum Freya comes here and marries me."

When Loki brought the news back to Thor, Odin and Freya, everyone was in shock. Freya was the queen of the gods – she couldn't go and marry a hideous giant!

That's when Loki made the suggestion that put Thor in a temper tantrum – and made everyone else chuckle uncontrollably.

"Thor just needs to dress up as Freya and go down to marry Thrym! It's a wedding tradition for the groom to give the bride his best hammer – so Thrym will have to give Mjollnir straight back to Thor!"

Now Thor was begging Freya: "*Please*, mother.

Can't you just go and *pretend* to marry him?"

But Freya shook her head. "Do you really worry more about looking like a girl than you care for the safety of your mother?"

At that, Thor looked at his feet. He mumbled, "Oh alright then. Where's your best dress?"

Thor looked very fetching in Freya's old wedding dress. Loki plaited Thor's hair to complete the look, then nearly knocked the mirror over by laughing so hard.

Thor snatched the mirror, looked at his reflection, and sighed. "Hopefully no-one will ever tell this story."

Freya came up behind him, and laid her hands on his shoulders. "My son, I hope they *do* tell this story. You are demonstrating something very important today: that it doesn't matter what you look like – it's what's in your heart that counts."

Encouraged by his mother's words, Thor stood. "Right! I'm off!"

Freya gently held his arm. "Not so fast. No bride would travel without a lady in waiting."

Loki kept laughing and laughing and laughing – until he noticed that both Freya and Thor were looking at him with smiles on their faces.

"What? Aw, *man...!*"

*   *   *

Thrym could hardly believe his eyes when he saw Freya and her maid walking down the paths of Jotunheim towards his cave. Thor and Loki looked so convincing that the giant really thought all his dreams had come true.

"Welcome Freya! I knew you'd come. You fancy me really, don't you – more than that old pufflehead Odin, I'm sure. Well don't worry! I'll look after you! As my wife, you won't have to do any work – except cook my dinner, pick my teeth, and scrub the sweat off my feet."

Thor hid his disgust behind a cheeky smile, and fluttered his eyelids. "Oo, Thrym, you big tease."

Thrym suddenly frowned. "My, Freya... what a deep voice you've got."

Thor froze. His mind buzzed. What could he say to that?

But Thor was the strong one – *Loki* was the clever one. In a high-pitched voice, he called up to Thrym, "All the better to speak to you with, your chiefness! My lady knew she needed a strong voice for you to hear her, so she practiced making herself as loud as possible. But she's got a bit of a sore throat because

of it!"

Thrym looked at Thor, and tilted his head to one side. "You tired out your voice for me? Awww... *Awww...* Aw Freya, I could almost actually love you for that. Come! Let's have a feast before our wedding!"

Thor and Loki sat opposite Thrym at a huge table. In the middle was an entire cow, eight plates of large salmon, and twenty bowls of salad and fruit. There were also tankards for everyone to drink some ale, which was waiting to be poured from a large jug.

Thrym was about to slice the cow to give everyone some beef to eat... when Thor picked it up and began biting off huge chunks! Thor had soon eaten the entire cow – after which he scoffed all eight salmon, polished off every bowl of salad and fruit, and gulped down every last drop of ale – from the jug!

Thrym blinked. "My, Freya... what an enormous appetite you've got!"

Thor realised he'd been a little too eager. He gave Loki a panicked look.

But Loki calmly looked up at Thrym. "All the better to look after you with, your chiefness! My lady has starved herself these last few days – not wanting to eat with Odin because she wanted to be with you, her true love. But now she needs energy to do all those jobs for you, like cooking and picking your teeth and scrubbing the sweat off your feet. So of course she needs plenty to eat!"

Thrym looked at Thor, and tilted his head to one side. "You went without food for me? Awww... *Awww...* Aw Freya, I might nearly actually love you for that. Come! Let's get married!"

The three of them went down to the beach, where some of Thrym's friends were waiting with a giant priest. Thrym and Thor stood side by side as the giant priest put garlands of flowers on both their heads.

Thrym turned to gaze into the eyes of his bride – then stepped back. "My, Freya... what huge *eyes* you've got!"

Loki quickly spoke up. "All the better to see you with, your chiefness! My lady was so excited about marrying you that she couldn't sleep for days – that's why her eyes are so red and wide. But now she can look at your handsome face every day, she'll sleep well I'm sure."

Thrym looked back at Thor, and tilted his head to one side. "You went without sleep for me? Awww... *Awww...* Aw Freya, I think I actually love you for that! There's only one thing I need to do for our marriage to be complete..."

At that, Thrym's best giant passed Mjollnir the hammer to Thrym, who passed it to Thor – and Thor raised it high...

Thrym gasped. "My, Freya... what gigantic *muscles* you've got!"

This time, Thor knew exactly what to say:

"All the better to *bop you over the head with!*"

With mighty Mjollnir in his hands, and his mother's wedding dress swirling around his legs, Thor bashed Thrym to the ground – along with the giant priest, the best giant, and all the other giant guests.

As Thor and Loki walked away, Thrym rubbed his head. "All I wanted was someone to cook my dinner, pick my teeth, and scrub the sweat off my feet...!"

Without looking back, Thor replied, "Just because I wear a dress, doesn't mean you can expect me to do *that*."

Loki smiled. "My, Thor... What a big attitude you've got."

Thor smiled back. "All the better to tell great stories with."

A DRESS

Knut finishes his story wheezing with laughter. Harald wipes his eyes.

I look at them both, a big grin on my face. I realise it's a long time since I've felt this happy. And then...

"*THAT'S IT!*" My cry makes them both jump.

Knut is first to recover from the shock. "*What's* it, Ethel?"

"Don't you see? That's the answer, right there in your story! What's the one kind of person that the monks are not just letting in, but actually *bringing* into the abbey?"

Knut's eyes widen. "Women!"

I nod, very excited now. "And girls!"

Out of the corner of my eye, I notice Harald

suddenly look to Knut, some kind of worried expression on his face. And Knut's voice has gone all serious: "Ethel – I can't let you go in there."

"Why not? I wouldn't be alone, would I."

Harald is frowning. "You wouldn't?"

"No! Don't you see? That's our disguise. We have to dress your uncle up... as a woman!"

There's a moment where they're both staring at me as if I've just turned into a real-life troll.

And then that wide, confident, joyful smile is back on Knut's face. He claps his hands. "Ethel, you genius! You've got it!"

Harald is shaking his head, but I see he's smiling too – he knows it's a good idea. He suddenly moves a little bit closer to me – almost as if he's going to congratulate me with a hug.

I quickly turn to Knut. "So, how are we going to do it?"

Harald stops mid-lean. He looks a bit awkward.

Knut muses. "What would we need to make me look like a woman?"

We get ready to write down some ideas, but our brains are beginning to get exhausted from all the thinking. Actually, maybe *you* can help with this. What do you think we could find to disguise Knut as a woman? Write your thoughts on the next page...

get A

Wig put it in

get a

DRESS put it on

DONE

Not all of the things on our list are in the abbey. Of course we all think Knut should shave – but when we find Abbot Alfsig and ask him for a razor blade, he can only produce the one he uses to shave the tonsures for new monks. My fingernails look sharper than that!

"Oh well," says Harald, with a bit of a cheeky tone. "Nobody said you had to be a *pretty* woman...!"

Still, eventually we have everything a king could need to look like a woman – including a woman's dress. Harald takes the head from an old grey mop to use as a wig. It's not the same colour as Knut's beard, but it works. Sort of.

Harald and I stand back to admire our work.

Knut stands there, shuffling his feet a bit. With a gruff voice, he asks, "How do I look?"

Harald shrugs. "Like a man in a dress."

I get what he means. Women's clothes don't look that much different from men's clothes. And there are men with long hair too.

I take a step forward. "Being a woman isn't just about your clothes, Your Majesty! It's about how you hold your body, how you move, how you sound."

Knut's eyes do that twinkly thing. And suddenly, he strikes a pose. With a rough, high-pitched voice, he asks, "How about now?"

My face is beaming. "Perfect!"

Knut claps his hands. "Excellent! Now, we have just one more problem to solve."

Harald and I groan. At exactly the same time, we both exclaim, *"Another* problem?!"

Knut nods. "We need them to capture us when *we* want to get captured – otherwise it could be a long time before our plan starts to work. So how can we get their attention? We can't just wander around the Fens until they see us – that could take days. And we can't just go up and knock on their door, either – they'd definitely find that suspicious..."

"Ethel could sing."

We both turn to look at Harald, and he goes a bit pink.

"You know – like she did earlier. No-one – I mean, no *monk* – could resist that sound."

Knut is nodding. "Brilliant idea, Harald!"

My face feels hot and red, then cold and white, all in the space of a few seconds. "How many times do I have to tell you? I don't sing for people!"

But Knut just grins. "Sing for the land, then, just like before. That will remind everyone what we're fighting for. Now, let's get some rest – when dawn comes, we'll be off to save the day!"

He summons a monk to show me to my room for

the night. We all say goodnight – but I feel like I'm already dreaming.

Is that it? Have I just agreed to sing in front of people *again?* And then let myself get captured by the horrible monks who stole my mum?

What am I *doing?!*

A Song

I can't sleep. It's not the rug on the stone floor – that's far more comfortable than my own rug on the damp wooden floorboards back at home. It's not the distant singing of the monks in their service for Compline – that's quite relaxing, really. It's not even the fact that, tomorrow, I'll be travelling alongside a king I only met this morning as he wears a dress in the hope of sneaking into an abbey full of wicked monks to see if my mum's still alive. The day has been so full of surprises that crazy sentences like that are starting to sound normal.

No. It's the fact that I'll be singing tomorrow. Singing in the middle of a marshy field. And I have no idea what I'm going to sing.

None of the songs I know seem right, somehow. So I've sat here, staring at this wooden tablet for ages, trying to think of a *new* song to write. But my mind is like that tablet: thick, dusty, and blank.

Not that it's important which song I use to get the monks to notice us, of course. It's just that the Viking army will be listening too, from their hiding places in the reeds.

Oh, alright. It's that *Harald* will be listening too.

Do you know any good songs? Perhaps you could help me write one over these next few pages...?

Over the marshy fields in
a boat with a king
called knut he is so
wild just like a flute —

un um ventricle

and P. lug

with no

YEAH

BOB BOB BOB
BOB^2 / BOOOB

Naming the Land

(properly this time)

Knut and I leave Saint Etheldreda's Shrine as the monks begin their service of Lauds. I'm glad I'm not a monk – I can't imagine going to church twice before the sun comes up – but the music along with the sight of the sunrise makes me catch my breath as we step into the boat.

I'm nervous, but the sight of Knut attempting to punt the boat in that dress is a good distraction. He looks ridiculous.

He stares off into the distance as he pushes the pole into the river behind him. So I ask, "Penny for your thoughts?"

He scratches his head, dislodging the mop a little. "I was just trying to think of a good name for this new united kingdom of ours. I really want it to be something great, something that brings everyone together. But I just can't think."

I look out at the fields that surround my beautiful home, searching for inspiration. "How about 'Greenland'?"

Knut chuckles. "That one's been taken by another Viking, I'm afraid! About forty years ago, Erik the Red found a land that was all white, and called it Greenland to persuade other Vikings to come and settle in it."

"What a colourful story! Were they all purple with rage?"

"I don't know, but they're all blue with cold now!" Knut giggles, then sighs. "I don't know how these serious discussions of ours keep ending up so silly, Ethel. But look – our journey is nearly over: I can see the abbey. Let's get ashore."

I help Knut drag the boat away from the river – well, I hold the boat while he does all the dragging, really – and then we start strolling through a field not too far from the abbey.

I can't help but stare at the stone walls, and think: my mum could be behind there.

Everything is silent – no Lauds here, just a lot of lazy monks who are probably only just stirring from their beds.

Knut puts his hands to his mouth and does a surprisingly good impression of a pheasant. He's answered by a lot of low twittering from the bushes that I'm pretty sure is not the dawn chorus. Knut's soldiers were sent to find their hiding spaces about an hour before we set off.

Now, Knut nods at me. It's time.

I take a deep breath, close my eyes, and... Nothing! The song I'd planned to sing has just disappeared from my head!

Knut is looking at me with a face full of concern. He whispers, "Ethel? Sing your song, Ethel. Sing the song you sang us last night."

Of course. I'll be confident with that one – I've done it before. I lift my chin and sing, letting my voice soar up out of the reeds like a heron taking flight and gliding low over the land...

We sailed across the seas,
Under rain and over foam –
Well, come hear the story
How the English found their home.

We found a land of green,
All around it we did roam –
Well, come hear the story
How the English found their home.

We all found our own corners,
Tried to build our homes alone –
But when wicked men came for us
We were overthrown...

'Til a good king bid us stand,

Side by side and hand in hand.

Welcome everybody –

Make yourselves at home in England!

I open my eyes and smile at Knut, waiting to see if he noticed that I changed that last verse. I'm hoping to see that inspiring smile of his. But instead, he's giving me a really strange look.

I don't know what to say. "What?!"

His expression doesn't change. "Where did that come from?"

"The last verse? I just made it up, didn't I!"

"Yes, but... Where did you get that idea?"

I'm rolling my eyes now. "Oh, come on. You *must* know that: I made it up about you."

Now Knut shakes his head a little. "Not that bit. I meant the last couple of lines – what were they? 'Welcome everybody, make yourself at home in'...?"

I frown for a moment, trying to remember. Then I realise. "Oh, *that?* 'England.' I meant to say 'the English land', but it didn't quite fit..."

That smile is back on the king's face. "Ethel, do you realise what you've just done?"

"What?"

"You've..."

His word fades out... and then he starts speaking hurriedly and loudly, in an ear-bashing high-pitched squeaky voice.

"You've woken up the monks! They're running for us! I think we're in *big trouble!*"

INTO THE ABBEY

Sure enough, three burly monks are making their way out of the little door in the abbey wall, grinning and nudging each other.

I recognise them – they're the same three that took Mum. The fattest one moves surprisingly fast over the grass, and I half expect him to lie down and roll towards us like a ball. He gets to us first, and grabs hold of my wrists so sharply that I can't help shrieking.

"The less fuss you make, the less I'll hurt you, little lady," he says with an unpleasant smile, and starts dragging me back up towards the abbey. Even though we want to get caught, the experience is horrifying and I can't stop myself from trying to escape. But the monk has me, and he's not letting go.

Looking behind me, I see that the other two have picked up Knut – one at his feet and the other with a hand over his mouth. Knut is hanging onto his slipping mop-wig while trying to make it look as if he's just clutching his head in despair.

Once inside, we're dragged through a cloister – a big square walkway. Several women are scrubbing the floor, and a few more are digging the garden in the centre – but none of them look up.

I don't think any of them is Mum.

A door leads off the cloister into a huge hall, where more large and lazy monks are sitting eating sausages for breakfast – served by more women. And there, in a huge wooden throne at the end of the hall, sits the Abbot.

Abbot Alfsig, leader of the monks at Saint Etheldreda's Shrine, was thin, old and slightly bent over – like an ancient tree. But *this* Abbot... He looks like a pig that's *swallowed* a tree.

As the monk flings me onto the floor in front of him, I notice he has five chins. His fat wrists, poking out of his robe, are each about as wide as my neck. And his hands are like cushions with dimples where the knuckles should be.

Knut huffs as he's thrown down on the floor beside me. I know he's the king. I know there are loads of Viking soldiers outside. But seeing this bully of a man in front of me, I can't help but feel terrified.

And I still haven't seen my mum.

The Abbot sneers at us. "Well, well, what have we here? Which one of our new pets is the song-bird? I'm guessing not the hairy one. Ugh, have you ever seen a woman so ugly?" He spits at Knut, then grins at the monks around us. "We'll start this one off sweeping the grates and chimneys, I think – perhaps all the ash will be good for her complexion!"

Knut strikes a pose and says, in a falsetto voice, "Oh, how horrid! How can you be so horrid?"

It sounds pretty silly. But as the Abbot turns back to me, I don't feel at all like laughing...

"As for you, you pretty little song-bird... Ha! The best place for a bird is in a cage. You'll hang above our heads here in the hall and sing for us at mealtimes. And if you do it very prettily, *maybe* we'll feed you some bird seed."

Every time he says 'bird', a drop of his spit hits me in the face, near my eyes. I can feel my hands making fists – if only I had my eel spear right now...

Still with the silly voice, Knut almost sounds as if

he's enjoying himself. "Oh, you horrid man, you can't get away with this! Just you wait until King Knut finds out what you're up to, you big bully!"

That makes the fat Abbot rock with laughter. "King Knut?! Ha! You hear this, brothers? This woman thinks King Knut might save her! *Ha!*

"All these slaves are English! Who's going to run to tell a *Viking* king that *English* women are in trouble? Why would a Viking king care about some English slaves? Even if he did – everyone knows monks are good Christians. Why would King Knut believe anyone saying some monks are behaving badly?"

Well, now Knut stands tall... He whips off his wig... And, from somewhere down the front of his dress, he produces his crown and places it on his head. "King Knut would believe it," he says regally, in his deep voice, "because King Knut sees it with his own eyes!"

The other monks gasp, and there's the sound of chairs scraping back on the floor – some of them are standing up, as if preparing to run.

But the Abbot only blinks for a few moments before sneering again.

"You may be here, King, but you should not have come alone." He looks to his monks and yells, *"Seize him!"*

Knut moves fast. He takes hold of his crown again, and raises it so that it catches the light of the sun. There's a bright, golden flash – beautiful, brilliant...

...and gone as soon as the monks grab Knut's arms, pinning them against his sides. I wait for the king to push them away, and start thumping lazy monks to the ground left and right. But he doesn't seem to resist. Because he doesn't want to? Or because he can't?

Now the Abbot's cackling again – and some of the monks are joining in. "What, were you going to offer me your crown in exchange for your freedom? You really are a stupid king – I'm going to take your crown anyway!"

Then the Abbot waves his hand. "Hurt him a little bit, boys."

One of the monks kicks Knut's leg. The other one hits him in the shoulder. It's so horrible, I have to look away. Where are the soldiers? Where's my dad? Where's my mum?

Then, I see it: an eel spear, being cleaned by a very old lady in the corner of the hall. They probably let her use it because she's strong enough to catch eels, but not quite strong enough to attack a monk.

But if I can get to it...

Suddenly I feel hands grasp both my legs – so

hard it brings tears to my eyes – and the fat monk from the field hisses, "Where are *you* going, miss?"

I look to Knut. The monks have taken a step back from him, and he's standing there clutching his stomach and squeezing his face.

My mind is racing: *where are the soldiers?!*

But then Knut straightens his back, calmly folds his arms, and gives me that smile of his. He is panting hard as he speaks, but he hides any other sign of being in pain. "Don't worry, Ethel... Remember... The light... From the crown..."

The Abbot is laughing so hard in his throne now that I wonder if the ground will start to quake. He is nearly shrieking with delight as he mocks Knut. "The light from your crown, king? What did you think that would do? Dazzle us to death?"

Knut shakes his head, just once. "No... Something else..."

The Abbot's nose curls as he glares at the king. "Well what then?"

Knut glares back. "You'll see... In about three... two..."

The Abbot prepares to release another vicious laugh – but, suddenly, there's the sound of a horn quite close to the other side of the door.

Knut twitches an eyebrow. "One."

Then there's a huge crashing sound as the Viking army storm into the hall with blaring horns, stomping boots, and battle cries.

Now the Abbot's rattled. He tries to get to his feet, but his giant behind is stuck in his chair – so he can only watch as the Vikings quickly fill the hall and surround all the monks. "Seize them all!" shouts Knut.

Most of the Vikings begin grabbing hold of the monks, but one of them rushes to stand by the king's side. As he thrusts his sword into the air, I recognise him – and I can't help but notice how his face is covered in a certain wide, inspirational smile.

He must get it from his uncle.

"For England!" yells Harald – and all the Vikings echo, "For England!"

Harald races over to me as the fighting starts. We share a high five – but then I cross my arms and scowl. "What took you so long?"

He shrugs my scolding away. "Hey, I knew these Fens of yours were soggy, but I didn't realise *how* soggy. I'm going to be scrubbing mud off my leg straps for weeks, I bet. Still – I think we got here about the time that Uncle expected..."

Just then, Knut passes us – holding a monk gagged and bound over his shoulder, who he deposits onto a growing pile of wiggling monks that lie like huge maggots around the throne of the Abbot.

The Abbot himself has been strapped into his chair. Knut approaches him – and, as the king starts to speak, the room goes quiet.

"Now, you nasty man. What shall I do with you?"

The Abbot wriggles and glowers – but there is real fear in his eyes.

Abbot Alfsig steps from among the Vikings and looks down his hook nose at the quivering man. "One thing is for sure: the bishop will be hearing of this. None of these unpleasant monks will be allowed to continue their pretence that they are holy men."

"Yes," says Knut, "but what would be the best punishment to fit this horrible crime? Chop a few of their heads off? Throw some of them into a pit of snakes? Force this fake Abbot to live without food for a whole year?"

The wicked Abbot bites his lip.

"Aha!" cries Knut loudly, and all the horrid monks jump and groan. "I know what I should do. I'll ask my chief advisor..."

I look at Harald. I wonder what the king's nephew will suggest?

But Knut doesn't ask for Harald. He calls *me*.

"Ethel? What do you think we should do with

these men?"

Of all the surprises I've had these last two days, this is the biggest – a room full of people waiting to see me, a poor English eel catcher's daughter, give advice to the most powerful Viking under the sky. "Me? Oh... Well..."

I look at the floor and hum to myself – but only for a moment. Because then, an idea pops into my head.

I walk up to the fat Abbot and poke him in the chest. "This man wanted to make women and girls into his slaves. So I think we should turn *him* into a slave! Him and his monks should build some new villages – villages where English and Vikings can live together in peace."

All the Vikings cheer. The feeling in my chest is simply incredible.

Knut declares, "What an excellent plan! And so it shall be done. Now: I believe we have one more point of order here before we depart..."

The Vikings step away from the centre of the room, the doors to the hall are pushed wide open, and in comes a tall, elegant woman. She smiles at Knut.

"Are you ready, my love?" she asks. "We have them all."

"Yes, my Queen, we're ready. Bring them in!" says Knut. He takes the lady by her hand and leads her over to me. "Ethel, meet my wife: Queen Emma. She and the wives and mothers of my soldiers have been busy going from top to bottom of the abbey while we've been in here and —

I can't hear the rest of what he's saying, because there – in the middle of the crowd of women now following Queen Emma into the room – I recognise a face.

"Mum!"

I run to her for the best hug of my life.

ENGLAND

That evening, we're back in Saint Etheldreda's Shrine at Ely. Abbot Alfsig has his monks serve a feast. King Knut and Queen Emma are at the head of the table, with Dad and Mum sitting on one side of them – and Harald and me on the other side.

As we eat, several Vikings come and pass wooden tablets to Knut. Each one has a suggestion for what to call the new kingdom – and each one is the same: *England.*

Knut piles them up behind his seat. "I think we have a winner!"

Harald winks at me. "We all heard you sing the name in your song, and we think it's perfect."

I'm honestly surprised by this. "Really? Even

though it comes from the word 'English'? You wouldn't prefer 'Vikingland' or something?"

Harald shrugs. "Hey, you English were here first. Besides, we already have Vikingland – that's basically what 'Denmark' means in your language. And, in a way, if we call this place England, then it means anyone who lives here can get to be English – even us Vikings. So we really can all be on the same team."

I realise I'm staring at Harald a bit. He's actually more thoughtful than he looks.

Then I remember his troll face with the cheese sticking out his mouth, and I get the giggles. Harald asks, "What?!" – but I'm giggling too hard to answer.

Mum leans her head on Dad's shoulder. "Thank you for rescuing me."

Dad huffs playfully. "It was nothing to do with me. It was your daughter. And the King, and his Vikings, and the monks here – but mostly your daughter."

They're both smiling at me, and Knut and Emma are too. My cheeks are burning.

Dad coughs. "Seriously, though – we couldn't have done anything without King Knut, his men, and these monks. I don't know how I'll ever repay them. The only thing I'm any good at is catching eels!"

Abbot Alfsig is sitting nearby. Hearing Dad, he puts down his cup. "Catching eels, you say?"

"Yes, Father Abbot. That's my trade."

"Well, then, there's certainly a way you can repay us here! Our new church will be built with eels!"

"Sounds slippery," I say. "I don't think they'll stay on top of each other."

Alfsig chuckles. "Oh Ethel! I meant we trade eels with the monastery at Peterborough for stone. We are *paying* for our new buildings with eels." To Dad, he adds, "So if you'd like a job here, I will happily name you Saint Etheldreda's Chief Eel Catcher today!"

Knut muses. "That's a shame, because I had a job offer for you as well, Legres. I was going to ask you to be mayor of the first new village that the rogue monks build. I'm going to call it Littleport, and it could do with some laws to help everyone get along together. What do you think?"

Dad shrugs. "Don't see why I shouldn't do a bit of both," he says. But then he looks at me and winks. "Especially when I've got a royal advisor in the family who can help me come up with a few laws for the new village. What say you, Ethel?"

Laws for a new village! Well. What sort of rules do *you* think we should have so that people can live happily and peacefully in the new village of Littleport? I'd love to have your help one last time – please write your ideas for laws over the page...!

LAWS OF
LITTLEPORT

Everyone has a job

£5 fine.

NO stealing but trading
is allowed £50 or 1
Prison depends what
steal.

No killing 50 year
sentence.

Mum squeezes Dad's hand. "That's you sorted, then!" she says, and grins at me across the table. "What about you, Ethel?"

I nudge Harald and smile. "You know what? I think I have a plan."

Knut leans forward with interest. "*Another* plan? Do tell!"

"Well, those monks are going to travel all over the land right? Building new villages and towns? So maybe they could also be useful for spreading the new name of England everywhere they go."

Queen Emma looks at me with a warm, radiant smile. "I see. And how will you make sure they do that?"

"By singing to them! Harald and I will sing to them while they work."

Harald gulps. "We will?"

Knut laughs heartily. "Ethel, you won't want to hear *him* sing! But he's pretty good at playing the lyre. Maybe he could accompany you."

It's Harald's turn to go a bit red. "If you want, Ethel..."

I grin. "Definitely! You can play the lyre, and I'll sing to those monks while they work. I'll sing my song about England over and over again, until it's so stuck in their heads that they can't help singing it themselves – and then they'll spread it wherever they go!"

Alfsig is beaming like a baby. "What a great idea! It is a very catchy song. Why don't you give us a performance of it now?"

So Harald fetches his lyre – and we do.

> *Now a good king bids us stand,*
> *Side by side and hand in hand.*
> *Welcome everybody...*

Bonus Features

Fact or Folklore?

The story of *The First King of England...
in a Dress!* is based on a legend called
The Eel Catcher's Daughter – which comes from
Cambridgeshire, a county in the old kingdom of East
Anglia.

This legend was first written down by a man called
Walter Barrett in 1963, but was told by storytellers
before then. One storyteller – a man called Chafer
Legge – even said he was related to Legres, the first
mayor of Littleport.

The original legend doesn't tell us the name of
the eel catcher's daughter, though it does say she
married a Viking prince. Knut had three sons, but
one of them would have been a baby at the time of
this story – and the other one wasn't even born yet!
Knut's only other son, Prince Sweyn, never married.
So if the eel catcher's daughter *did* marry a Viking
prince, it was probably Knut's nephew Harald.

Before 1963, there's no written record of any monks kidnapping women in 1017. But then, who wrote nearly all the records in 1017? Monks!

However, there *are* records by some monks from a town called Ramsay (a Cambridgeshire city) which say Knut got upset with them in 1017, and wanted to throw them out of their abbey. The records don't say why. Perhaps the monks were trying to hide their naughtiness from going into history books...

There are also records of Knut paying visits to the area, including one which tells how he heard the monks of Ely singing as he rode a boat along the river – and he really did make up the song that you read here in the chapter called *To Ely*.

Whatever the truth, the village of Littleport is definitely still there today. The legend says Knut called it "Littleport" because a port is a stopping place by a river – and you'll find Littleport along the river just a few miles north of Ely. Even some of the roads in Littleport are named after the legend – for example, Crown Street is named after the way Knut attracted the attention of his Viking soldiers from inside the abbey.

Even if the legend is *not* true, it does still tell us something important: English people liked Knut. Because they didn't write stories down in 1017, they had to share them by telling them to their friends – and they would only do that if they liked the story. Since this story shows Knut being a good guy, they must have also liked him!

This is important because it gives us a clue about where England really came from. We don't know for sure if Knut brought all the seven English kingdoms together and called them England because he heard Ethel sing it in a song. But we do know that Knut was the first king to be called "King of England", and we also know that – after Knut became king – English and Viking people stopped fighting for the longest time in history since the Romans.

So England was probably created because Knut managed to get the Vikings and the English all working together. Don't you think that sets a good example for the whole country?

To find out more about where England came from, look out for a book called *Who Made England?: The Saxon/Viking Race to Create a Country*. And you can read *The Eel Catcher's Daughter* along with other local legends in a book called *Cambridgeshire Folk Tales for Children*. Both these books were written by Chip Colquhoun, who helped write the book you're reading now!

About the Characters

King Knut

Nobody knows exactly when Knut was born, or who his mother was. But historians do know that his father was King Sweyn Forkbeard of Denmark, who took Knut with him to fight the English armies in 1003AD – after the English king killed a lot of Viking people, including Knut's aunt.

If Knut was fighting in a Viking army in 1003AD, he was at least ten years old. That may sound too young to be a soldier today, but Vikings would join the army as soon as they were strong enough to pick up a sword!

King Sweyn's fight with the English went on for ten years, and Sweyn eventually won – but he died soon afterwards. The English king who killed Knut's aunt then came back to the land – so Knut returned to Denmark to build a bigger army. He didn't need it that much, though – when Knut returned to the English kingdoms of Northumbria and Mercia, he found the people there were happy to let him be king without a fight!

The other English kingdoms weren't so easy, though, and Knut kept fighting English soldiers until 1016. Even though he could have killed the last English king, Edmund Ironside, Knut decided to make friends with him – so it was only when Edmund died that Knut became king of the last English kingdom, Wessex.

Before Knut, all English kings had called themselves things like, "King of Wessex", "King of the English and Northumbria", or just "King of All the English". But in 1018, Knut decided to call himself "King of England". This was probably the first time the word England was used by a king – so it seems Knut must have helped create the new country of England.

Knut married Emma in 1017, and they had two children: a son called Harthaknut and a daughter called Gunhilda. Emma was Knut's second wife – his first wife was called Elfgifu, who had two sons with Knut: Sweyn and Harold.

Knut ruled England quite peacefully, and became well known as a ruler across Europe. His daughter Gunhilda married the most powerful man in the world, Emperor Henry III.

Knut also gave his nobles a rule that they needed to treat everybody the same, whether they were rich or poor. In those days, not many kings said this – in fact, William the Conqueror got rid of this rule when he took over England in 1066. The rule didn't come back to England until King John's Magna Carta in 1215 – that's nearly 150 years later!

But Knut was a successful army leader too. By the time he died in 1035, he was also the king of Denmark, Norway, and parts of Sweden. English royals didn't rule such a large area again until King James I started the first British Empire around 1607!

Knut's name actually means "nut". Perhaps this was the perfect name for him: he was a very hard nut to crack!

THE EEL CATCHERS: LEGRES AND ETHEL

At the time of this story, eel catching was the main job of people living on the flat marshy lands of the Fens in East Anglia. Eels could be caught using multi-pronged spears like the kind you saw Ethel using in this book. But really, the spears were a back-up – the main way to catch eels was with an eel trap.

The eel catcher would leave a bait in this bulge-shaped wicker basket, knowing the eels would find it easy to get in – but they'd have a very hard time getting out!

Most English furniture in 1017 was made with wood – including bits of driftwood from Viking shipwrecks! If Ethel had any toys, she would have made these herself out of wood too. Because they had no paper, any writing they did was carved into wooden tablets – but most people (adults as well as children) weren't clever enough to read or write.

Most English homes in this time had just one room – Legres is lucky to have a separate kitchen! That one room would include a fire for cooking and keeping warm, some rugs for sleeping, a table for eating, and a pot for "you know what"...

Once Knut became king, more towns and villages began getting built around East Anglia – including the village of Littleport. Legres may well have been the first mayor of Littleport, but he may also have been the last – Littleport doesn't have a mayor anymore. Perhaps Legres was just so good that they didn't think he could be replaced!

About the Stories

The stories told by Knut and Ethel are both old and new...

Old: Thor's Stolen Hammer

You can find this story in *The Poetic Edda* – a big collection of the Vikings' favourite stories.

New: The Coalminer and the Frost Giant

This tale is full of Viking mythology – Vikings certainly enjoyed stories about frost giants. But it was actually created from scratch by Adam, Ewan, Jacob and Denzil from year 4 in St Andrew's Primary School, Soham, who told it to the authors of this book in 2016!

OLD: THE POTION OF POETRY

This is another story you'll find in *The Poetic Edda*. But if you read it there, you'll find the characters all have slightly different names – including Great Hunter Woden, who is called... Odin!

Confused? Well, don't worry: there's an easy explanation as to why an English girl like Ethel would know a Viking story. You see, both English and Viking people came from the same part of the world: *Europe*, around the area we now call Germany. They were known as "Germanic tribes", and most of these tribes had similar stories – the characters just had slightly different names.

NEW: KEKU THE FROG

In old English mythology, a lot of gods looked like (or could turn into) animals. So this does sound like the kind of story an English girl like Ethel would have known about 1,000 years ago... but was in fact born in the brains of Nick, Mark and Oskaras from year 3 in Millfield Primary School, Littleport, who told it to the authors in 2016!

However, the old English didn't actually have a frog god – so Chip named the frog-man after an Ancient Egyptian god instead.

NEW: THE WITCH WHO HATED HILLS

Ethel's song, which she sings when Knut first discovers that she's a girl, is based on a story by Sophie from year 4 in Littleport Primary School – which was told to the authors in 2016.

In Sophie's original tale, the witch's land-flattening rampage was ultimately ended by a magical baker called Isabel and her giant gingerbread man. And it's a good job the witch *was* stopped – otherwise the flat Fens may have covered the whole country!

About the Storytellers

Amy Robinson

Amy has been telling stories ever since she could speak – in fact, she didn't speak at all until she was ready to speak a complete sentence! She studied English at the University of Cambridge, where she met Chip – and they had fun writing, directing, and acting in musical plays together.

She then trained to be a teacher, but soon decided she wanted to be a storyteller instead. She called Chip and asked him for help creating Snail Tales. That was in 2007, and both Amy and Chip have been telling stories professionally ever since.

In 2011, Amy became one of the faces of the Oxford Reading Tree, telling stories like *The Little*

Red Hen and *Rumpelstiltskin.* You can watch these videos for free by visiting

www.oxfordowl.co.uk/storyteller-videos

In addition to her work founding Snail Tales, Amy is the children's worker for her local group of churches (known as a "benefice"). She has written 3 books on puppetry and storytelling produced by Kevin Mayhew Publishers, and regularly provides scripts and materials for GenR8 – a Cambridgeshire charity running free Christian assemblies and events in schools.

Amy spends her spare time writing poetry and attempting novels. She lives in a rectory in Suffolk with the rector, two children, two guinea pigs, and too many puppets to count.

CHIP COLQUHOUN

Chip wrote his first story before anyone had taught him to write! It was just a series of squiggles, so no-one knows what it was about – not even Chip. But it already had punctuation, like full stops and paragraphs – so Chip definitely knew what writing was all about.

He wrote several plays whilst at school, and a few more when he went to the University of Cambridge – which is where he met Amy, and started working on shows with her. Chip's first experience of storytelling was when Amy invited him to join Betty Stubbens Musical Entertainment Group, which visited care homes around Cambridgeshire to share songs and stories with the folks who lived there.

So Chip was very happy to help Amy create Snail Tales. In 2011 he also became one of the faces of the Oxford Reading Tree, telling stories like *The Big Carrot* and *The Magic Paintbrush*. You can watch these videos for free too by visiting

www.oxfordowl.co.uk/storyteller-videos

Since then, Chip has told stories in 7 countries, written the EU guide to storytelling in schools, and directed several theatre shows – including *The First King of England... in a Dress!* He's also written two collections of folk tales both published by The History Press; and also *A Little Sport in Littleport,* originally published by Babylon Arts and now available as an ebook from Snail Tales.

He lives in Cambridgeshire with his partner Emma and kitten Tito.

DAVE HINGLEY

Dave has always loved drawing and comic books. Since studying animation at the University of South Wales, he has worked in and around animation for the last eighteen years – but in the last few years, he has enjoyed creating illustrations for books and theatre shows.

One of Dave's posters received an award from the National Operatic and Dramatic Association in 2014. He has also produced illustrations for both of Chip's books published by The History Press to date, and artwork for the stage show *The First King of England... in a Dress!*

He lives in Cambridgeshire with his fiancée Vicki – unless you're reading this after November 2017, in which case he lives there with his *wife* Vicki!

How We Wrote This Book

Two storytellers, one book... So how did *that* work?

Well, it began with Chip choosing to add the legend of *The Eel Catcher's Daughter* to his collection of *Cambridgeshire Folk Tales for Children*. The original legend didn't have Knut dressing up as a woman, but Chip liked the idea of Knut catching the monks red-handed – and the legend of *Thor's Stolen Hammer* gave him the perfect idea for how to do this. Chip liked the story so much that he decided to turn it into a theatre show – and so was born *The First King of England... in a Dress!*

Chip wrote the script for the show, but even that wasn't all his own work. First, he went into some local primary schools to help them create brand new stories from scratch in storytelling workshops – and that's where he heard stories from the children mentioned in *About the Stories* above.

Not only that, but quite a lot of what Knut and Ethel said in the script was actually first made up by the actors: L-J Richardson as Knut, and 11-year-old Olivia Balzano as Ethel.

Chip then gave the script to Amy, who began turning it into a novel. Amy liked the idea of telling the story from Ethel's point-of-view, and adding in extra bits of local legend – such as Ely Cathedral being built out of stones bought with eels. But there was one big problem with the script: in it, the storytellers speak with the audience a lot, even getting their help to capture the monks at the end!

So Amy and Chip spent time working out how to put the story in a book, while still giving *you* the chance to join in. To do this, scenes were added which you won't find in the show – such as the argument between monks and Vikings in Ely Cathedral.

Amy then went away and wrote most of the novel – sometimes using the speech from the script, sometimes changing it... and many times making up brand new speeches! Meanwhile, Chip wrote the stories that Knut and Ethel would tell each other.

Above – The cast of the original stage production of **The First King of England... in a Dress!** From left to right: Olivia Balzano (who plays Ethel); Chip Colquhoun (who plays the Storyteller and Legres); and L-J Richardson (who plays King Knut).

And, at the same time, illustrator Dave Hingley began drawing the pictures that you find all around this book.

Finally, Amy and Chip sat down with all the bits of the story, read it through, and checked it all worked – together with the pictures. Sometimes little bits needed to change – for example, Dave might have added some details in his pictures that Amy and Chip hadn't thought of, but which needed to go into the writing so everything matched up.

All-in-all, everyone had great fun putting this book together – and we hope you've had fun sharing it with us too!

Have fun with *your* storytelling!

Welcome to the end of the book!

We'd love to know what you thought
of it. Please let us know by going onto
the website of your favourite bookshop
(e.g. Amazon) and leaving a review.

Not only will your review help us write even
better books in the future, but it may help
someone else decide whether to buy this book!
So if you can leave a review,
we'll be hugely grateful!

Enjoyed this book?

Then we'd like to share
another one with you... for *free!*

All you need to do is join our mailing list.
Not only will you get a short ebook for free,
but we'll also send you the occasional
free story, links to free storytelling videos,
news about when we're storytelling near
you, special offers on new books and CDs...
– and no spam ever.

You won't get many emails from us,
but the ones you get will be fun!

Simply visit
www.snailtales.org/freebook
– and make sure you have
your grown-up with you.

PS: Share this with your teacher, and you
might get to see us in your school!

We look forward to sharing more
stories with you soon!

Join in the story!

See THE FIRST KING ~~OF ENGLAND~~ *in a* DRESS! *...live!*

A family storytelling spectacle with puppetry, music from an Anglo-Saxon lyre, and ***plenty*** of joining in!

Ask your favourite local theatre to email us on **shows@snailtales.org**, and we'll make sure you get free tickets *and* a show soundtrack when we visit!

Thank Yous

Amy, Chip and Dave would like to give huge thanks to...

...**Olivia** and **L-J** for bringing our characters to life at theatres and festivals across the UK, and **Nathalie**, **Emma**, **Peter** and **each venue's technical and front-of-house staff** for the important contributions they make too. Plus, of course, all those who come to see the show – we couldn't do it without you!

The **Arts Council of England**, **Arts Development East Cambridgeshire (ADEC)** and **Cambridgeshire Libraries**, who all helped us develop the original stage version of *The First King of England... in a Dress!*

...**norse-mythology.org, Wikipedia** and **Ely Museum** for helping us with our research.

...Amy's husband **Tiffer** for tea breaks and boat trips.

...Chip's partner **Emma** and his father **Paul** for dinners and TV catch-ups.

...Dave's fiancée **Vicki** for being a fabulous mum-and-wife-to-be.

...**Nicola at The History Press**, whose commissioning of Chip back in 2015 to write *Cambridgeshire Folk Tales for Children* was the initial spark that led to this stage show and novel.

...**Dr Maureen James** for passing on WH Barrett's original version of The Eel Catcher's Daughter tale in her book *Cambridgeshire Folk Tales*.

...and **the Association of Christian Writers** for their support, advice and encouragement – especially **Wendy** with her helpful tips on printing and publishing.

ALSO BY AMY ROBINSON

PUBLISHED BY KEVIN MAYHEW PUBLISHERS
Performing with Puppets

Tales from the Jesse Tree:
25 Bible stories to watch, tell and explore

Follow Me!:
A Daily Lent Guide for Families

ALSO BY CHIP COLQUHOUN

PUBLISHED BY THE HISTORY PRESS
Cambridgeshire Folk Tales for Children

Who Made England?:
The Saxon/Viking Race to Create a Country

PUBLISHED BY SNAIL TALES
A Little Sport in Littleport

PUBLISHED BY
THE EU LIFELONG LEARNING PROGRAMME

"Something Bad Has to Happen":
Storytelling & Creativity in the Classroom
for Enhancing Educational Development

For details on how to get copies of any of these
titles, please email **books@snailtales.org**

Snail Tales in Schools

Comparative studies have shown that children remember 25% more when taught through storytelling than rote learning – whilst growing in confidence, concentration & creativity too.

See how Snail Tales could work with your school by visiting **www.snailtales.org/schools** – and mention this book to get a special **£50 off** our visit!

9 781999 752309